DEATH IN MONTMARTRE

A Paris Booksellers Mystery

Evan Hirst

Copyright

www.evanhirst.com

February 2016

ABOUT THE AUTHOR

Spurred on by a passion for history and a love of adventure, Evan Hirst is an award-winning screen writer who has lived and worked all over the world and now lives in Paris.

Evan's *Paris Booksellers Mysteries* plunge into the joys and tribulations of living in Paris, where food, wine and crime make life worth living… along with a book or two.

She also writes the *Isa Floris* thrillers that blend together far-flung locations, ancient mysteries and fast-paced action in an intriguing mix of fact and fiction aimed at keeping you on the edge of your seat.

A Little Paris Christmas Murder is a holiday short story in *The Paris Booksellers Mystery* Series.

Find out more about Evan Hirst's books at
www.evanhirst.com

CHAPTER 1

Standing at her outdoor book stand on the Quai Malaquais in the center of Paris, Ava Sext, a tall, reed-thin woman in her late twenties with dark hair, a heart-shaped face and warm brown eyes that flashed whenever she smiled or frowned, pushed a wayward strand of hair behind her ear and gazed across the river at the Louvre. She sighed with contentment as the *bateaux mouches*, the flat-bottomed glass-topped tourist boats, drifted slowly by on the Seine below.

Paris was in the throes of the dog days of summer -- those hot, sultry days that stretched out with no end in sight.

Today, the sun was shining high overhead in the bright blue sky, just like the day before and the days before that. Eternity was unfolding at a snail's pace, if at all.

There was something dreamlike about Paris in August. It was the city of love at its picture postcard best. Days like this were why people moved there. As most Parisians were off on holiday, the city's hustle and bustle gave way to a slower village-like pace.

Ava had grown used to the enduring sameness of each day and had started structuring her days in a similar manner.

Every morning, after a leisurely shower, she would have coffee at "her café" -- Café Zola. There she would catch up on neighborhood gossip, or lack of such, as there wasn't much going on.

Afterwards, she would cross the street and unlock, one by one, the heavy metal padlocks on her stand's three bottle-green wooden book boxes and marvel at how fortunate she was.

A year earlier, Ava had been working for a boutique PR firm in London, writing social media posts for celebrities. Someone had to do it... and that person was Ava. On call 24/7, her budding career had come crashing down when she drunk tweeted on a client's account after a bad breakup.

Now she was a "*bouquinist*": a bookseller who sold used books out of the boxes that lined the Seine in the center of Paris. Since 1859, concessions to the boxes that ran on from the Pont Marie to the Quai de Louvre on the right bank and from the Quai de la Tournelle to the Quai Voltaire on the left bank had been granted by the city of Paris to a lucky few.

Ava was one of that select group.

She had taken over the stand following the death of her Uncle Charles. Charles Sext, a New Scotland Yard detective, had quit his job after an inheritance and moved to France, having decided to enjoy life far from crime and criminals, although that hadn't kept him from solving a few cases between book sales.

Sleuthing was in his blood, just as Ava had discovered it was in hers when she worked on a few cases with Charles's friend and fellow bookseller, Henri DeAth.

As a bird made wide loops high in the sky, Ava wondered if Parisian criminals went on holiday in August. She imagined a beach filled with policemen and criminals enjoying the sea, side by side. No one in their right mind would pull off a crime on a glorious sun-drenched day like this.

As eternity continued to unfold around her, Ava removed a leather bound book from her stand. *Swann's Way,* written by Marcel Proust, was the first of seven volumes that made up *In Search of Lost Time.* The books captured Proust's memories of his childhood and coming of age in late 19th century France. Clocking in at 4,215 pages, reading the books would be a fitting homage to an endless summer.

Ava strode over to a green and white lawn chair set up

under a tall tree, sat down, opened the book and began to read.

And then in a split second, everything changed.

A leaf drifted down from the tree overhead and landed on the open page. Ava picked the leaf up and examined it. It was green, but there was a clear yellow tinge around its edges. While its fall had been silent and swift, the leaf's message couldn't be clearer -- summer was almost over, and the endless days were ending.

Fall would soon be there.

And in France, fall meant *la rentrée*, the start of the new school year.

However, in Paris, the rentrée was much more than that -- it was the start of everything. Museums would have new exhibits. Cinemas that had been showing golden oldie classic films all summer would screen films fresh from the Cannes and Venice film festivals.

And overnight, as if by magic, every Parisian woman would have bought the new season's must-have accessory.

Ava, a Londoner born and bred, had never experienced a sea change like this in the UK. There, summer was summer, fall was fall, and never the twain would meet.

Filled with a sudden sense of urgency, she put her book down and walked back to her stand. Knitting her eyebrows together, she examined the book boxes and the books in them. While some booksellers on the quays specialized in art books or crime books, Ava was a generalist. You might find a guide to knitting Easter bunnies next to a text on Buddhism. Most of her books were in English and French, with the occasional German or Italian book thrown into the mix.

Running her eyes over the rows of books before her, she was struck by the utter lack of order.

Her stand was chaos.

Pure chaos.

In a sudden burst of zeal, Ava began pulling books from the boxes and piled them up on the sidewalk. When the rentrée came, her stand would be organized and ready for business.

She separated the books into fiction and non-fiction. Fiction books would be alphabetized by author. Non-fiction books would be organized by topic. Infused with a frenzied energy, she moved books from pile to pile.

As she sorted through them, she was astonished by what she found. Where in the world had a guide to competitive bubblegum blowing come from? And while *The Autobiography of a Zombie* had a certain ring to it, she was unsure whether to place it in fiction or non-fiction. At a loss, she stuck it in the self-help section.

Someone would buy it.

The one thing she'd learned as a bookseller was that there was a buyer for everything. Absolutely everything… even *The Autobiography of a Zombie.*

An hour later as sweat dripped down her forehead, Ava had almost finished alphabetizing her fiction books. Holding an oversized fiction book by Anatole Aart in her hand, she frowned.

Could she put an oversized book as the first book in the A section?

Impossible.

She stuck it in the back under R. Anyone with an average level of intelligence looking for a book by Aart would certainly check under R, if they hadn't found it under A.

Feeling someone staring at her, Ava looked up.

Ali Beltran, a tall tousled-haired man was watching her, bewildered. Ali, a trim man in his early-thirties who wore heavy black-rimmed glasses that made him look serious and hid his wicked sense of humor, ran the stand next to Ava's along with his twin brother, Hassan. Ali was a prize-winning painter who had graduated from the prestigious Paris school of arts, the *Beaux-Arts* Academy. As usual, he had a sketchbook in his hand.

"What are you doing?"

Ava raised her eyebrows. "Organizing."

"Is there any reason for such a rash decision on one of the hottest days of the year?"

"The rentrée is coming. When it arrives, I'll be ready," Ava announced as she held *Squirrels of France* in her hand. The animal section was the logical choice for the book, but she didn't have one. Inspired, she stuck the book in hobbies.

Ali shook his head in dismay. "The rentrée is a media creation. You know how I deal with it?"

"How?"

"I don't," Ali responded with a grin.

"That isn't true. Your gallery show is at the end of

September so you're as much of a victim as I am."

Ignoring her remark, Ali opened his sketchbook and began to sketch.

"What are you doing?"

"Capturing a hard-working bookseller in action," Ali replied, continuing to draw.

"Make that a gorgeous hard-working bookseller in action and I'm all in…"

"That goes without saying."

Ava continued to organize her books. As she started in on a towering stack of non-fiction books, her resolve flagged. She sighed loudly.

Ali put his sketchbook down. "Want some help?"

Ava gave him a grateful smile. "I'm dying for help. I'm not a born organizer if you hadn't noticed."

"I noticed," Ali said as he came over and picked up a book. "*German Cooking for Beginners!*"

"Cooking!" Ava repeated. Not finding a cooking section, she stuck it in foreign travel.

"*Biking in Paris!*"

Ava hesitated between sport and Paris. She chose the latter.

Thirty minutes later, they were done. Like a proud mother hen, Ava inspected her stand.

"How's Nate?" Ali asked as he picked up his sketchbook and began drawing again.

"Nate is Nate." Ava said, not knowing what that meant. Nate Rosier was the man she was dating. A production manager for international films that she had met on her last case, Nate traveled all over the world for his job. At the moment, he was in Italy working on a film. She had called him early that morning, and he still hadn't called her back. *Out of sight, out of mind*, Ava thought, more miffed than she would like to admit.

"Isn't he in Rome?" Ali asked as he walked around Ava studying her from different angles.

"Living the *dolce vita*." Ava frowned when a troubling thought popped into her mind. "Is there a reason I always date men who live or work far away?" Nate was the second of her French boyfriends to live or work abroad. For all she knew, she was the one driving them out of the country.

Ali began to draw again. "You like your freedom and attract men who like theirs. It's a win-win situation."

"You think so?" Ava said, not entirely convinced. "What if it's me?"

Ali shook his head. "It's not you. The day you want someone who will never leave your side, you'll find that person in a flash."

Ali's answer cheered her, although she wasn't sure that she wanted someone who would never leave her side. It sounded suffocating.

Ali made a few quick strokes of his pen and handed her his sketchbook. "*Et voilà*!"

Ava studied the drawing with dismay. The woman didn't look anything like her. Ava considered that her up-do was effortlessly chic, while the woman's hair in the drawing was a mess. The woman also had a crazed expression on her face. "This isn't me!"

"It's the inner Ava. It's a lovely drawing," Ali countered. Noticing the book on her lawn chair, he went over and picked it up. "*Swann's Way*… You're reading this?"

"Before I realized the rentrée was coming, I was. Now I

might just leave it to next summer."

Suddenly, Ali's face lit up. He pulled out his cell phone and scrolled through it. "Here it is! I knew I had it!" Ali said holding up his phone, triumphant.

"*In Search of Lost Time*?" Ava asked. "Why would you read a book that long on your phone?"

"No one would. This is the *Proust Test.*"

Ava's eyebrows went up in recognition. "Like the one in women's magazines?"

Ali nodded. "Back when Proust took it, it was a parlor game... I'll get us some iced coffee, and we'll take the test together."

Sipping the iced cardamom coffee that Ali was famous for, Ava leaned against the tree as Ali read the questions out loud as he squatted her lawn chair.

"Where would you like to live?" Ali asked.

Ava gazed up at the Louvre across the way, then moved her eyes toward Notre Dame Cathedral further up the river. "Here!" Ava answered without hesitating. "Paris is the most beautiful spot in the world. And you?"

Ali pursed his lips in thought. "Paris is my first choice, but I wouldn't mind spending time in Tahiti. For Gauguin... and the landscape. Painting there would force me to use a different palette."

"How did Proust answer the question?" Ava asked.

Ali smiled. "In the country of my ideal!"

"Poetic but vague," Ava replied, finding Proust's answer wanting. "Next question."

Ali ran his finger down the screen. "Your favorite occupation?"

"Occupation as in a hobby?" Ava questioned.

"Exactly."

"Selling books and sleuthing" Ava replied.

"Sleuthing and bookselling aren't hobbies. They're your jobs," Ali corrected.

Hearing his words, a thrill ran through Ava. Being a bookseller-sleuth in Paris was something she never would have imagined in a million years. Yet here she was doing just that. Life was full of surprises. "What about you?"

"People watching and sketching," Ali said. "People are fascinating. When I observe them from afar, it gets my mind going. I start sketching, and paintings spring from those sketches."

Ava pointed to his drawing of her. "Just don't get inspired by that."

Ali laughed. "I never take a whole person. Just a nose here, an eye there...In your case, I might make an exception and take a nose and an ear."

"Be my guest. What was Proust's favorite occupation?" Ava asked.

"Reading, dreaming and writing verse."

"I wonder what Nate would answer?" Ava asked, wondering again why he still hadn't called her. Had he met a pretty Italian? Film shoots were a hotbed of romance.

Ali pushed his glasses up his nose. "My guess is that he'd say solving puzzles."

Ava's eyes widened in astonishment. "Puzzles? Nate works in film!"

"Film production is one giant puzzle with lots of different pieces that have to go together. That's why you two get along so well... You solve crimes. Crimes are a puzzle. Why do people read mystery novels? They want to solve the crime and be smarter than the sleuth."

Ava groaned. "A smart sleuth? That's not me... I always get it wrong as a reader. I've read *Death on the Nile* by Agatha Christie three times. Each time, I forget who did it."

"Proust would have said that you and Nate were looking for infinite truths in a sea of possibilities," Ali teased.

Ava shook her head in mock indignation. "Clearly, Proust never worked as a sleuth. One last question..."

"The qualities you most admire in a woman..."

Ava answered without thinking. "Intelligence, spark and a sense of humor. But I'd say the same thing for a man. What did Proust say?"

Ali checked his phone. "Gentleness, naturalness and intelligence."

Ava shook her head in disagreement. "Gentleness gets you nowhere."

"Don't forget that he answered this at the end of the 19th century," Ali responded.

"I don't believe things have changed that much," Ava protested, sure of what she was saying.

Ali burst out laughing. "Spoken like the hard-nosed feminist you are." Eyeing his stand, Ali raised his chin. "It's time to work." He ripped Ava's portrait out of his sketchbook and handed it to her. "In honor of Proust!"

Ava took her portrait and studied it. With a sigh, she removed the pins from her up do and let her hair fall around her shoulders. The drawing was proof that not everyone was born to be effortlessly chic.

Before Ali could walk away, his phone rang. He answered it. "Henri? Aren't you in Bordeaux for a wedding? That's odd. Montmartre? I'll tell her." Ali hung up and slipped his phone in his pocket.

Ava raised her eyebrows. "Henri's still in Paris? Is he alright?"

"He's appraising a book collection. He wants you to meet him at the bottom of the funicular that goes up to Sacré-Coeur Basilica."

"Now?" Ava asked, astonished.

"Now," Ali said.

"Why didn't he call me directly?"

"He did. You didn't answer."

With a frown, Ava checked her bag. Her phone wasn't there. Now she knew why Nate hadn't called her back. All at once, something struck her. "Why would Henri cancel a wedding in Bordeaux to appraise books? Couldn't it wait?"

"Apparently not," Ali said. "Don't worry about your stand. I'll keep an eye on it." He picked up *Swann's Way*. "I haven't read this since high school. I might give it another go."

CHAPTER 2

As the taxi sped north from the Seine toward Montmartre, Ava barely noticed the cool breeze coming through the window or the jazz music playing on the radio. Her mind was focused on one thing: *Why had Henri chosen to appraise books rather than go to a wedding in Bordeaux?*

Henri had been looking forward to the wedding as a chance to catch up with friends and family. Instead, he had stayed in Paris on one of the hottest days of the year to go through shelves of dusty old books.

There was nothing urgent about appraising books. The books wouldn't be going anywhere, and any potential buyers wouldn't be back until September. It made no sense, and everything Henri did made sense.

A shiver of anticipation ran through Ava: *Could the appraisal have to do with a crime?*

Henri DeAth had not only been her uncle's best friend and a fellow bookseller, the two men had worked on several cases together.

But Henri was more than a bookseller and sleuth, he was

also a former French *notaire*, a notary. In France, a notary was a member of a powerful caste. They were wealthy, secretive and protective of privileges that went back hundreds of years. Henri had once joked to Ava, "Not only do we know where the bodies are buried, we helped bury them…"

A French notary giving up his practice before he was in his dotage or dead was as rare as a snowstorm in August.

Impossible.

However, Henri was that snowstorm. In fact, he was a blizzard.

He had come to Paris from Bordeaux, a city in southwestern France, hub of the Bordeaux wine-growing region, to deal with a tricky inheritance and had never left.

At a mere sixty, he had sold his practice to his nephew and moved to the French capital. Ava's apartment, the bookstand and Henri's Parisian house had all come from that. However, Henri's roots in Bordeaux were deep. If he had chosen a book appraisal over a wedding there, something major was in play… theft, blackmail, maybe even murder!

Cheered, Ava looked out the window.

As the taxi crossed the busy Boulevard de Rochechouart and

drove into the small narrow streets that criss-crossed Montmartre, the atmosphere changed instantly.

The geography and street layout meant there were few cars and no buses. Merchandise spilled out onto the sidewalk from the discount clothing shops and fabric shops that lined the steep narrow streets.

The neighborhood was more colorful and lively than the 6th arrondissement where Ava lived.

While each Paris neighborhood had its own distinct atmosphere, Montmartre was in a world of its own. It still possessed the authentic charm and village-like atmosphere that it was famous for at the end of the 19th century. Back then, Van Gogh and Toulouse-Lautrec would spend their evenings sipping absinthe in Montmartre's dark bars or frequent raucous cabarets before winding their way up the hilly streets to their furnished lodgings.

Even today, Montmartre's steep windy cobblestone streets exuded a whiff of bohemia. Lively theaters, cabarets and wine bars vied with trendy restaurants and art galleries for the attention of passersby. Montmartre even had two windmills and a vineyard that produced wine.

Looking out the taxi window, Ava was in heaven. It was

a perfect day to come to Montmartre even if there wasn't a crime that needed solving…but she hoped there was.

CHAPTER 3

The taxi zigzagged through the narrow crowded streets and screeched to a halt at the bottom of the funicular that went up to Sacré-Coeur, the basilica that stood on top of the butte Montmartre, Paris's highest hill. As Ava paid the driver, she gazed up at the big white church. No fan of its architecture, she frowned in disapproval.

"Each time I see it, it looks more and more like a giant Byzantine meringue," Henri joked as he joined her. "I half expect someone to take a bite out of it."

Happy to see Henri, Ava grinned. "If it weren't for Sacré-Coeur's location, tourists wouldn't rush to see it. Now what is so urgent about a book appraisal?"

"We'll soon find out," Henri replied with an enigmatic smile.

With a raised eyebrow, Ava stepped back and studied Henri's appearance. Always casually elegant, today he was wearing dark jeans and a pale grey shirt that made his salt and pepper hair and blue eyes stand out. He was far too well dressed for crawling around dusty books. "Is there something you didn't mention?"

Henri nodded. "I should have told Ali. Garance invited us for lunch first."

"Garance?" Ava asked as she instinctively checked out her own clothing: a grey and silver T-shirt dress and light grey sneakers. Chic and comfortable. Totally appropriate for any occasion.

"Garance Pons," Henri replied and fell silent.

Ava hid her annoyance with Henri's cat and mouse game. *Why didn't he just come out and tell her who Garance was and what was going on?*

She knew the answer.

If Henri did that, he wouldn't be Henri.

It just wasn't French.

"She's a notary?" Ava asked.

"Yes. She's part of that dangerous breed."

About to explode at the lack of information, Ava took a deep breath. "What did she say that convinced you not to go to the wedding?"

The expression on Henri's face became serious. "She said it was urgent. I've never heard Garance use the term before. I didn't even know it was in her vocabulary."

Ava burst out laughing. French notaries were notorious for taking their time and doing things by the book. She couldn't imagine any notary thinking something was urgent, even if it was.

"The apartment we're going to is up near the Sacré-Coeur," Henri added, pointing towards the basilica.

Frowning, Ava eyed the long line of tourists that snaked up to the entrance to the funicular. "We're going to have a long wait."

"We're not taking the funicular. We're walking up."

Incredulous, Ava stared at the steep steps that led up to the top. "In this heat? We might have a heart attack."

Henri gestured to the tall trees and old-fashioned lamp posts that lined the steps. "People come from all over the world to see these steps and take pictures on them. Somehow, they survived. I assume we will, too."

Silent, Ava glared at Henri.

"If you like, I'll take your picture."

"That won't be necessary," Ava responded.

"Or you can take mine," Henri said as he walked to the steps.

Irritated, Ava dragged behind Henri, hoping that he was wasn't serious and would opt for the funicular.

Henri pointed at two Japanese teens taking selfies. "We could ask them to take our photo together."

Ava ignored his remark and gripped the iron railing that

ran along the steps. "How long have you know Garance?" Ava had met several of Henri's friends from Bordeaux but had never heard him mention Garance.

"Forever…" Henri said. "Thirty years, at least. Ironically, the last time I saw her was at a wedding in Bordeaux."

Ava nodded. In France, it made perfect sense that you would invite your notary to your wedding. The notary would be there for you until the end, and even after... For all she knew, there might even be a special section in heaven for French notaries to continue their work. "Did someone die?" Ava asked, ingenuous.

Amused, Henri raised his eyebrows. "Why do you think someone is dead?"

Ava tapped the side of her nose. "Intuition."

"One of her clients," Henri said as he continued climbing the stairs, sidestepping an Asian bride and groom having their photo taken by a professional photographer.

"I knew it!" Ava exclaimed with a grin. She had just passed the first test of Sleuthing 101: get to the heart of what is going on.

"Don't you think you're becoming a bit ghoulish?"

Ava shook her head. "Not at all. My interest isn't personal. It's professional."

Henri slowed, took out his phone and scrolled through his photos. He stopped at one, held it up and compared it to the building on the side of the steps next to them.

Ava peered over his shoulder at the photo. "What's that?"

"If I'm not mistaken, Garance's client took his last breath where you're standing."

"That's not funny…" Ava replied, instinctively scooting up two steps in case Henri wasn't joking.

Henri narrowed his eyes and looked around. "It was late. There was a rainstorm. Her client was either going up or down the steps. No one knows. He slipped and fell. There weren't any witnesses because of the weather. When he was found, he had been dead a while."

"An accident?" Ava asked as her sleuthing mind kicked in.

"That's what the police concluded."

Ava crossed her arms. "What do you think?"

Henri looked at his watch. "I think we should hurry as Garance is waiting for us."

"Henri, did anyone tell you that you can be annoying at times?"

Henri chuckled and continued walking.

When they reached the top of the steps, Ava spun on her heels and glanced down. The steps were steep. It wouldn't take much to slip, hit your head and die… especially on a rainy night. The steps were so worn that you could even slip on a day like today if you weren't careful.

So far nothing proved that Garance's client's death was murder. But then nothing proved it wasn't…

Ava smiled. Things were looking up.

CHAPTER 4

The building was a six-story 19th century building with a red inlaid brick façade. Henri typed in the code, and the heavy front door swung open. In the cool entrance hall, Henri checked the names on the mailboxes and groaned.

"Let me guess," Ava said. "It's on the top floor."

Henri rolled his eyes around the hall. "And from what I can see, there isn't an elevator."

Ava followed Henri up the steep wooden stairs. Except for the sound of their footsteps and the creaking of the worn wooden stairs, the building was silent. No doubt its residents were on holiday. When they reached the top floor, Henri stopped and caught his breath.

"I'm not as young as I thought I was," Henri said, gripping the railing.

Her legs aching, Ava noted that Henri hadn't even broken a sweat on the walk up while she could hear her heart pounding.

Henri took a deep breath, stood up straight and strode across the landing to a dark blue door and knocked. The door swung open immediately. A striking woman in her fifties with long blond hair pulled back in an effortlessly chic makeshift chignon smiled when she saw her visitors.

"Henri!" Without hesitating, the woman stepped forward, hugged him warmly and kissed him on the cheeks. She turned to Ava. "I'm Garance Pons… One of those horrible notaries that Henri probably warned you about."

Henri burst out laughing. "You're painting me in a bad light."

Instantly at ease, Ava grinned at the woman. "Henri's convinced me that not all notaries are dull. I'm Ava Sext."

Garance nodded. "You run a book stand near Henri's." Garance waved them in. "Look around while I bring lunch out. I'm so hungry I could eat a horse."

"Can I help?" Ava asked. Garance was not at all what she had expected. The woman had dark grey eyes that were lined with smoky green eyeliner. Her clothing and jewelry were classic yet ultra trendy at the same time. She looked more like a literary star than a notary.

"No, thank you. Everything is ready. Take in the view. It's magnificent," Garance said as she disappeared into the kitchen.

Turning, Ava caught her breath. The view from the apartment was spectacular. The apartment had a panoramic view of the city. Light flooded into it from all sides. It would be a bowl of light even on the darkest Parisian day. The owner of the apartment was a lucky person… except that he was dead.

Henri walked from one end of the room to the other, gazing out the windows. "I'm impressed. Really impressed." He turned to Ava. "And you?"

Ava eyed the city before her. "I'm in awe. Who could guess from the street that an apartment like this was hidden inside?"

"Paris is full of surprises. That's part of its charm. You open a door or enter a courtyard, and you might be in another century." Always the professional, Henri strode over to the bookshelves that covered the walls opposite the windows and ran from floor to ceiling. There were thousands of books on them.

Ava gaped at the number of books. "We have our work cut out for us."

"But with a view like this, it will be a joy to do," Henri responded as he took a book off a shelf and paged through it.

Garance entered the room and placed a crispy roast chicken with potatoes in the center of a round marble table set for three. A green salad, bread and a carafe of wine were already on the table. "What do you think of the apartment?"

"I'm astonished. The view is spectacular," Henri replied.

Garance pivoted and eyed the room. "David Rose, or DR, as everyone called him, had fabulous taste in everything."

Her words appeared to send a message to Henri. Instantly, he strode around examining the sculptures and paintings that were scattered around the room. "Including expensive art?"

"Including very expensive art," Garance replied. She held up the wine bottle. "I opened the wine and decanted it before you got here."

Henri took the bottle from her. "A 2012 Chateau de la Tour Clos Vougeot Grand Cru? That's an expensive choice for a simple lunch."

Garance reared back in false indignation. "Simple lunch? This is a chicken from Bresse. The greens are all organic, and the bread is from the Poilâne bakery… Yes, it's a simple lunch, but it's up to your standards, Henri," Garance said, teasing him. She turned to Ava. "Even when we were younger, Henri always ate well. When other students were eating sandwiches, he'd find some inexpensive bistro where you ate like a king for nothing."

Henri looked nostalgic. "Sadly, the days of eating well for nothing are over." He picked up the wine bottle. "How did you get your hands on a treasure like this?"

"DR owned a wine shop. However, he was also a wine broker on the international market for high-end bottles. He gave me several bottles of expensive wine at Christmas last year and told me to save them for the right occasion." As sunlight spilled through the windows, it made the wine in the carafe glisten. Garance looked at Ava and Henri. "I believe this was the right occasion."

Henri picked up her carafe and poured wine into the glasses. He handed Garance and Ava a glass, and took one for himself.

With a sad smile, Garance raised her glass. "To DR!"

"To DR!" Henri and Ava repeated.

Ava sipped her wine. It was wonderful. In fact, it was one of the best wines she had ever drunk. It was too bad that DR had to die for her to taste it.

As everyone ate, Ava listened as Henri and Garance caught up over lunch. In France, it would be considered impolite to discuss an urgent matter while eating. Food was serious. Business was left for later.

As Henri refilled everyone's wine glasses, Garance turned her attention to Ava. "You're British?"

"From London," Ava confirmed.

"I adore London," Garance said with an envious smile. "The city has so much energy. I would have loved to work there, but my notarial office is here."

Ava leaned forward, curious to learn more about the elegant woman before her. "How did you become a notary?"

Garance sighed. "Like in a fairytale… The choice was made for me in the cradle."

"Your father was a notary?" Ava guessed.

Garance nodded. "And my grandfather and his father before him. I'm an only child. If I'd had a brother, I would have been spared and might be living in Chelsea now."

Henri suppressed a laugh. "Being a notary isn't exactly like working in a coal mine."

Garance smiled at him. "I'm not complaining. I know I'm lucky. I like my work. I like my clients… most of them."

Henri kept his eyes on Garance. "And DR?"

"DR was a wonderful person," Garance said sadly.

"But he had secrets?" Henri asked in a gentle probing manner.

Garance shrugged. "More than most French people? I can't say."

Ava raised an eyebrow. "Do all French people have secrets?"

"That's the very essence of being French," Garance replied. "But with reality TV, those days are ending. Happily or unhappily…"

"How did you meet DR?" Henri asked as took a bite of his salad.

"At his wine shop… The French Corkscrew. It's at the bottom of the butte near the Marché St. Pierre," Garance explained.

Ava nodded. The Marché St. Pierre was a famous fabric store not far from the funicular. You could buy discounted fabric of all types including couture fabric. Ava's couch had a swath of brocade over it that she had bought there. She liked to think that the rest of the brocade had been made into a couture dress for a Gulf princess or a South American socialite.

Garance sipped her wine. "I was curious about the shop. It was always closed. Hours weren't posted. One day I strolled past it, and it was magically open. I went in. DR and I hit it off right away. He explained that the shop was a hobby. He only opened it when he felt like it. We talked for hours about everything and nothing. It's rare to find someone with such a breadth of interests. Plus, he was charming. Although at times he could be ornery. "

Henri leaned forward. "Ornery enough to kill?"

"That's for you to tell me," Garance replied, staring into Henri's eyes.

Henri waved his hand at the apartment. "Did he inherit this?"

Garance shook her head. "No. He bought it six years ago."

Henri couldn't hide his astonishment. "Six years ago, prices were sky high. It must have cost a fortune."

Garance clasped her hands together. "It did cost a fortune. It belongs to a holding in Singapore."

Ava watched Henri. She could see the thoughts running through his mind.

"Did DR inherit money?" Henri questioned.

Garance shrugged. "I don't know. I've only known him three years." She sat back in her chair. "Let me tell you what I do know. DR was in his mid-fifties. I always thought he was much older. He was someone who stepped directly into late middle age. He often played the role of the absent-minded professor lost in the world of wine. I wasn't fooled. He was as sharp as a tack. I didn't know about his life as an intermediary selling high-end wine when I met him."

"Aha! The secret, at last..." Henri said, all ears.

Garance stood up and grabbed some magazines from a side table. Ava recognized them immediately. They were famous American wine magazines.

Garance opened the first magazine to a page she had bookmarked and handed it to Henri. "This is DR at a Sotheby's wine auction in New York two years ago."

Ava stood up and walked behind Henri to view the pages with him.

"DR is the man wearing glasses on the left," Garance explained.

Ava studied DR. He was the type of man you would walk past and not notice. There was nothing about him that stood out. He was of average height and average looks. Even his clothing looked average. He looked much older than he was.

Garance opened another magazine. "Here's DR at a famous restaurant in NY for a tasting of Burgundy Grand

Crus. The other guests were Asian millionaires and US tech moguls. They drank hundreds of thousands of dollars of wine that evening." She opened other magazines to bookmarked pages of tastings in Hong Kong or London. DR was in every picture.

"For an absent-minded professor, DR certainly got around," Henri said as he studied the photos.

Garance sat back in her chair. "DR traveled first class. He stayed in five-star hotels. His clothing was bespoke. Even his shoes were handmade. I found correspondence between DR and his shoemaker requesting that his shoes look lived in, not new."

Henri put the magazine down on the table. "How did you get involved with him professionally?"

"After four or five meetings, I felt like we'd known each other for years. As I said, he was charming, although his charm crept up on you. It wasn't a charm that swept you off your feet. Two years ago, he asked me to draw up the papers for a wine foundation he was creating. I drew them up, he signed and everything was set to go..."

Henri frowned. "And then?"

Garance shook her head. "And then nothing. Everything came to an abrupt halt. When I asked him why, he said his money was tied up. I began to believe he was exaggerating his wealth. But then, I'd never seen this apartment, and I had no idea of this," Garance said pointing at the magazines.

Ava was fascinated. DR sounded like a man who had lots

of secrets… exactly the type of man who ended up dead.

"What do you know about his accident?" Henri asked.

"Nothing until Maître Longlet, his notary, called me about the will."

Henri was astonished. "You weren't his notary for the will?"

"No. In fact, I knew nothing about it. I was astonished that DR had named me executor of his will and as director of a holding company in Singapore that appears to have nothing in it except this apartment, his shop and a hundred thousand pounds, " Garance said.

"Did you accept?" Henri asked.

Garance's expression darkened. "Yes. If DR wanted me to be the executor, there was a reason for it. I intend to find out what that is."

Henri remained silent, but his expression was troubled.

Garance eyed him. "I know what you're thinking. How did he live like he did? How did he pay for it? When I drew up the papers for the foundation, he told me that he had lots of money set aside. If there is money, I haven't found it yet."

"That doesn't mean it doesn't exist," Henri said.

"Exactly," Garance replied with a determined nod. "We need to find it."

Ava couldn't contain her curiosity any longer. "Why did you need to see Henri today? What was so urgent?"

Garance reached behind her and grabbed a folder. She opened it and took out a paper with an email printed on it. "This."

Henri took the email from Garance and read it out loud:

David Rose invites you to an exclusive tasting of Domaine de Kirjac wines at his shop on August 12th at 7:30 pm. I promise you won't be disappointed.

Henri handed Ava the paper. She read the email and studied the email's details. It had been sent three days earlier from David Rose's email account.

"How could DR send an email if he's been dead for months?" Ava asked.

Garance's face clouded over. "That's my question."

"Perhaps he preprogrammed the email, and his account sent it off automatically," Henri suggested.

"Maybe, but I'm not convinced," Garance replied. "One, it was sent three days ago. We're in August. Even if he were alive, that's short notice. Did he really expect everyone to drop everything and come? Most people are on holiday."

Ava glanced at the email's recipient. "Who is Solange Vitrang?"

"DR's friend, a Burgundy wine expert and someone who helped him with tastings from time to time. When she received the email, she immediately contacted me. I met her when I drew up the foundation papers."

Henri's mouth fell open. "You weren't invited to the

tasting?"

"No," Garance said with raised eyebrows and an expression that spoke more loudly than any words could. "I wasn't."

"Tell us about Solange," Henri said.

"Early thirties. A stunning blond. Charming and intelligent. She wrote her thesis on Burgundy wine. She also wrote a very well-respected book on the region's post-war history."

Ava's face lit up. The French expression "*cherchez la femme*"... "*look for the woman*" ran through her mind.

Henri beat Ava to the punch. "Love interest?"

Garance laughed. "No. Not at all. I only saw them together two or three times. It was a meeting of minds. He enjoyed her knowledge, and she enjoyed the access. She didn't come from Burgundy."

Henri eyed Ava. "Burgundy is an even smaller world than the Bordeaux wine world. It's very difficult for an outsider to gain entry."

"But an outsider who is a woman makes it virtually impossible," Garance added.

Ava was surprised. "Surely things are changing."

Garance shook her head. "Burgundy is very traditional, very patriarchal. Give it another fifteen to twenty years, and things might evolve. When I took over my father's practice after his death, some of my father's clients changed notaries because I was a woman."

Annoyed, Henri drummed his fingers on the table. "France can be ridiculously traditional at times."

"When Solange received the email, she called me. She didn't know what to do. She forwarded it to me. After I read it, I told her to come and do the tasting. She should be in Paris by now," Garance said.

"She doesn't live here?" Henri asked.

"She lives in Brussels. She has a small *pied-à terre* off the rue des Abbesses," Garance said.

"Does she know you're the executor of DR's will?" Ava asked.

"She does. I didn't tell her. She just knew," Garance added. "Of course, DR could have mentioned it to her… But I would have preferred that he mentioned it to me first."

Henri read the email again. "I don't like this."

Garance's eyes flashed. "Nor do I. That's why I called you."

"What do you want me to do?" Henri asked.

"Go to the tasting. See who turns up. And then tell me what you think," Garance replied.

Henri was astonished. "You're not going?"

Garance shook her head. "The only person from DR's circle I've ever met is Solange. No one knows the terms of

DR's will, not even Solange. I intend to keep it that way."

"Who are we?" Ava asked.

"People brought in to appraise his books," Garance replied.

"Tell me more about Solange," Henri said.

Garance shrugged. "When we drew up the papers for the foundation, DR wanted Solange to have a leading role in it although he never formalized those wishes."

Henri was deep in thought. "Nothing was written in his will about Solange.

Garance shook her head. "Nothing."

Ava was surprised. "Don't you find that strange?"

Garance raised her chin. "A little. But it's stranger that he wanted me to be the executor and run the holding."

Henri picked up the email. "Domaine de Kirjac. That rings a bell."

"Domaine de Kirjac is an outrageously expensive, highly rated, impossible to get Grand Cru Burgundy. DR had a special allotment each year that he sold to his special clients."

Henri took a last sip of his wine. "Let me guess It's so rare that everyone invited will appear?"

"Everyone. You can fly to Paris from anywhere in the world in seventy-two hours," Garance replied. "Some will come for the wine. Others might appear to discover why a dead man invited them to a tasting. I know I would."

"Any doubts about his death?" Henri asked.

Garance bit her lip. "It's hard to say. It was a rainy night. It was dark. DR often took the steps up or down to his shop. It's possible he fell…"

"But it's possible that he didn't?" Ava asked as her mind spun into overdrive.

Garance nodded. "It's possible that he didn't. I'm off to Singapore this afternoon to find out more." She stood up and took two sets of keys off a hook on the wall and handed them to Henri. "Here are the keys to the apartment."

"Did you look in his computer?" Henri asked.

"I would have, but I didn't find it," Garance said. "A warning…"

Henri fell silent.

"Marc Virgile, the owner of Domaine de Kirjac is well-known for being incredibly abrasive."

Henri nodded. "Forewarned is well-warned. Did you search the apartment?"

Garance shook her head yes. "I looked everywhere for something that would tell me where the money was or what happened to DR. I didn't find anything. If you find something, let me know…"

"Immediately if not sooner… Spoken like a true notary," Henri said with a laugh.

Garance smiled at both Ava and Henri. "I have a plane to catch. Leave the dishes in the kitchen. My cleaning lady will do them tomorrow morning."

Henri stood up and kissed Garance tenderly on the cheeks. "You can count on me."

Garance grabbed her bag and gripped Ava's hands warmly between her own. "Keep an eye on Henri. I wouldn't want anything to happen to him."

CHAPTER 5

Looking out over the city, Henri sipped an espresso that he had made in DR's very expensive Italian espresso machine.

"What do you think?" Ava asked as she paced around the room.

"It's pure heaven. Whenever I drink espresso like this, I vow to get a fancy machine. Then the next day comes, and I stick with my small espresso maker. Maybe some day…"

Ava furrowed her brow. "I meant about the case."

"We don't know if we have a case or not," Henri replied. "What we do have are shelves and shelves of books to catalogue…"

"Which might or might not hold the key to what's going on?" Ava asked with a gleam in her eye.

Henri shrugged. "There's a slight chance we'll find a clue in one of the books… But there's an even better chance we won't. This isn't a mystery novel."

Ava walked over to a vase on the desk and peered inside it. It was empty. "There are millions of places DR could have hidden something in the apartment."

Henri finished his espresso and put the cup down. The spoon clattered against the porcelain saucer. "What do you think he hid? The name of the person who killed him?"

"We don't know that his death was an accident. People do fall down steps," Ava said, tit for tat. She crouched down, picked up a colorful cushion on an armchair and searched beneath it. Not finding anything, she put it back.

Henri looked at her with astonishment.

"What is it?" Ava asked, noticing the expression on his face.

"I expected you to jump right on the murder wagon."

Ava raised her eyebrows in mock outrage. "You make me sound like I'm on the prowl for a murder to solve. I'm not. Even on a dry day like today, the steps were worn, I easily could have fallen. So if DR was in a hurry, and the weather was bad, the chances of his slipping were high. But..."

Henri ran his hand through his thick salt and pepper hair. "But?"

"But Garance asked you to come because she believes DR's death was suspicious. In addition, dead men don't email."

Henri flashed a grin. "I like your down-to-earth Anglo-Saxon take on it."

"And I don't believe for a moment that he programmed

his emails before his death that was...?"

"Three months ago."

Ava shook her head. "Impossible. DR didn't send the email."

"I agree," Henri replied, rising to his feet. "Shall we start?"

As Henri opened and closed books at random, Ava strolled around the room trying to gain insight into the dead man. DR's taste was eclectic. Art Deco vases and oriental rugs were displayed alongside modern art. Kilim carpets in bright colors were piled high in the corner next to drums from Bali. She moved over to the bookcase. There were books on every subject from art to politics. Some were new. Some were old. She took a few books out randomly, paged through them and put them back.

"The books don't seem valuable."

Henri looked up from a book he was examining. "The appraisal is just a pretext for us to be here and learn more. When people meet us this evening, they'll ask questions. We're obviously not high-end wine buyers. It's best to have a cover story ready. Plus, the books will also give us insight into DR. From what I can see, he was interested in many things just as Garance said. Oddly, I haven't seen many wine books."

"Garance said she didn't find his computer. Who could have it?"

Henri shrugged. "Any number of people. Don't forget that Garance didn't learn about DR's death for a month. Someone with a key could have come here or gone to his shop and taken it."

Ava's eye lit up. "Or it could have been stolen when he fell on the steps. The person who sent the mail didn't need DR's computer to do that… only his password."

Henri lifted a Diptique scented candle off the shelf and brought it to his nose. "*Feu de Bois* -- Wood Fire… DR was a man after my own heart."

Ava walked over to the marble table. "I suggest we do the dishes. That way, Garance's cleaning lady only has to put them away."

"Good idea," Henri said. He picked up the salad bowl and wine glasses and carried them into the kitchen. Ava followed with the rest of the dishes. They scraped the dishes and put them in the dishwasher. When Ava went to throw out the wine bottle, Henri stopped her.

"Leave it. I'm keeping it as a souvenir…"

"Of a murder?" Ava asked, puzzled.

Henri picked up the bottle and studied it. "Of an incredible lunch."`

Ava was not surprised by his remark. Above all, Henri appreciated good food.

"I suggest we examine the kitchen. It might give us some insight into DR," Henri said putting down the bottle.

"The way into a man's psyche is through his stomach?" Ava joked.

Henri didn't respond. He opened the refrigerator. It was empty except for mustard, mayonnaise and mineral water. He opened the freezer and took out the ice cubes trays. He examined them before putting them back. "Nothing here."

Ava walked around the kitchen opening and closing cabinets. The contents resembled that of 90% of all French kitchens: olive oil, *herbes de provence*, *fleur de sel* salt, and different types of vinegar… There was a large coffee table cookbook on a wooden stand. Ava opened it. A recipe fell out. She stuck it back inside.

Henri was going through the dish cabinets. There were very few dishes. "I didn't see any dishes in the living room. That means DR didn't give large dinner parties… "

"Or ordered take out," Ava said.

As the dishwasher hummed, Henri strode down the hallway. "Let's look in the bedroom."

DR's bedroom had floor to ceiling windows with a view of Paris. The bed had a white embroidered throw on it. Brightly colored silk pillows were scattered on the bed. Books were piled high on a bedside table. Ava browsed through them. There were recent fiction books in French and English… nothing that would shine a light on DR. A pair of reading glasses was next to the books. Looking at them, a wave of sadness swept through her. It brought home that the apartment belonged to a real person, a person who would never return.

Henri swung open the door of a large custom made wardrobe. Inside, DR's clothes was perfectly arranged. Shirts, jackets, trousers and handmade shoes were in rows, separated by color. Henri went through the wardrobe and pulled a suit jacket out.

Henri held it up and studied it. "This is a handmade jacket, but there's no label on it. If DR took it off, no one would know who had made it. However, the cut would give away that it was bespoke. The ultimate snobbery..." Henri put the jacket back and picked up a pair of shoes and examined them. "Berluti... DR liked the best."

"Obviously, he had the means to buy the best. He traveled in style. He bought expensive clothes. If that's the case, where did the money go?"

Henri raised his eyebrows. "Maybe DR lived beyond his means. However, Garance would have told us if he had debts. The wine world is a tough world. Somehow, DR worked his way into the upper strata. That needs looking into," Henri said as he put the shoes back in the closet.

The longer they stayed in the bedroom, the more anxious Ava felt. She half-expected DR to appear and ask why they were searching through his belongings. "What time is the wine tasting this evening?"

"7:30. I wonder who will be there," Henri said, closing the wardrobe.

"At least one person who has a reason for holding the tasting," Ava responded as she headed to the door.

"And the others?"

"Someone who knows something or has something the person who sent the email wants. Otherwise, why hold a tasting?"

Back in the spacious living room. Henri sat in a swivel chair, and spun himself towards Ava. "What have we learned so far?"

"DR didn't entertain large groups... at least not here," Ava replied. "Not enough dishes."

"His taste in books is eclectic. Most of the ones I opened had been read. And there are no wine books that I could see."

"That is curious," Ava said with a frown.

"And where's the wine?" Henri asked. "The only bottle I saw today was the one we drank. Surely, he would have had a few bottles at home."

"Maybe he kept them at the shop?"

"Or someone might have removed them." Henri stood up and began pacing back and forth. "One... DR died. Two... The police investigated and declared his death accidental. Three... Some time after that, his notary learned about the death and contacted Garance."

Ava eyes lit up as she followed Henri's train of thought. "But that took time. In the interval, someone could have come here or to the shop and removed items they didn't want found."

"We'll never know. But the tasting tonight suggests that

DR's death left a problem to be solved… Just what that problem is remains to be seen."

"We might learn something at the tasting," Ava said. She was more excited about participating in the tasting than she would admit. She had tasted wine at the local wine shop but suspected that it did not compare with a professional tasting with high-end wines. And tonight's tasting was more than a tasting… it was a tasting with a hidden purpose. "Do you think the murderer will be there tonight?"

Henri burst out laughing. "So now it's a murder."

Ava looked sheepish. "We don't know that it's not… "

"If it was, there's a good chance that the murderer will be there," Henri confirmed.

"What should we wear?" Ava asked.

"To catch a murderer?"

"For the tasting…." Ava replied with a frown. Wearing the right clothing to an event was important in France. Clothes make the man… or in her case, the woman.

Henri eyed her clothing. "You could wear that… But if we're tasting reds, you might want to wear a dark color so as not to stain it."

"I have the same dress in navy blue."

"Problem solved." Henri eyed the bookcase. "I suggest we leave the books for another day. I need a shower and time to think before the tasting." He pulled out his phone and opened the taxi app.

"You don't want to walk down the steps?" Ava teased.

Henri grinned. "I've lived dangerously enough for one day."

As he called for the taxi, Ava picked up one of the magazines with DR's picture in it. She rolled it up and stuck it in her bag. She intended to do some research before the tasting.

CHAPTER 6

The French Corkscrew, David Rose's wine shop, was located on a quiet street at the base of the Butte Montmartre. At exactly 7:15, the taxi came to a halt down the street from the shop, and Henri and Ava climbed out. Henri was dressed simply in ironed jeans, black suede slip on shoes and a pale blue shirt that was open at the collar. Ava was wearing a navy blue dress with large pockets and flat black sandals with gold trim. A bright pink leopard chiffon scarf completed the look and matched the polish on her toes.

Looking around, Henri turned to Ava. "Ready when you are."

Checking the time on her phone, Ava stared at Henri, puzzled. "We're early. Is there a reason for that?"

Not only was arriving early in France frowned upon, Ava had never known Henri to arrive anywhere early, just as he never showed up somewhere fashionably late as was the habit with most Parisians. Henri always arrived on time, like clockwork, which wasn't surprising for an ex-notary.

Henri shook his head. "This isn't a dinner party, Ava. I have a tactical reason for being early, I'd like to speak with

Solange Vitrang before the others get there."

Ava feigned mock horror. "I didn't want to start off the wine tasting with a *faux pas*."

Henri laughed. "We French can be a bit unforgiving towards social blunders. Fortunately, society is changing."

They walked down the street. When they reached the wine shop, Henri tried the door. It was locked. Ava peered through the window that was partially blocked by a shade that had been pulled half-way down.

"Do you see anyone?" Henri asked.

"No one."

As there was no doorbell, Henri gave three short loud knocks on the door and waited.

A few seconds later, a tall, slim woman in her early thirties dressed entirely in black appeared in the back of the shop. Her long blonde hair hung loose. She hurried to the door and unlocked it.

"We're the first ones?" Henri asked as he entered the shop.

"Yes. I'm Solange Vitrang," the woman gushed, out of breath.

Henri held out his hand. "Henri DeAth. My friend is Ava Sext."

Solange did a double take on hearing Henri's last name. "*Death* like in English?"

"It's Flemish. The pronunciation does surprise people. I've gotten used to it over the years," Henri explained with a warm smile.

Solange smiled. "I'm glad you could come on such short notice."

"It isn't often that someone holds a tasting from beyond the grave," Henri replied.

Solange stepped backwards as if slapped. "I'm sorry. I'm not over DR's death. To be honest, I was as surprised as you about the invitation."

Ava studied the woman. Henri's words had shaken her.

Solange lowered her voice and stared at the entrance. "I half-expect DR to come through the door at any moment. When did you receive the email?"

Ava shook her head. "Garance asked us to come."

Henri smiled. "We're appraising Mr. Rose's books, and Madame Pons thought we'd be interested in coming to the tasting."

Ava winced. *Faux pas* number one… She shouldn't have used Garance's first name. Ava didn't doubt that she would make other ones before the evening was over.

Hearing that Garance Pons had sent them, Solange's entire attitude changed. Her hazel green eyes clouded over and she fell silent. Clearly, she didn't believe that they were telling her the whole story. "Let me show you the shop before the others arrive."

Solange locked the door as Henri and Ava stepped inside.

The shop was cool. Its walls were lined with old-fashioned dark wood shelves. Bottles of wine were lined up on them like soldiers going to war. A round wooden table stood in the middle of the store. Open wine bottles were on it. Henri approached the table and picked up a bottle. It was a 2003 Domaine de Kirjac.

"This is a very special wine," Henri exclaimed. "I'm honored that Madame Pons asked us to come. How many people did Mr. Rose invite?"

"I have no idea," Solange confessed. "The email didn't have a CC on it." Solange stared at Henri. "I'm glad Garance sent you. I was surprised when she said she couldn't come. I didn't want to hold the tasting on my own."

Henri raised his eyebrows. "Why?"

Nervous, Solange pushed her hair behind her ears. "I had a presentiment that I should cancel the tasting... that it would bring about disaster. I hope I'm wrong." She stared at Henri and Ava. "I don't understand why DR would plan a tasting for the middle of the month of August and prepare the email months ago. For all I know, there are no other guests… just us."

Ava leaned over the table to read the labels on the other bottles. They were all covered with paper. "It's a blind tasting?"

Solange nodded. "The owner of the vineyard requested

that."

Solange took the wine bottle from Henri, covered the label and put it back on the table. "We're lucky to be tasting these wines. They're rare. This is the first time I've done a tasting for the vineyard."

"David Rose did them?" Ava asked.

Hearing DR's name, sadness spread across Solange's face. "DR did them. I wasn't invited. They were for big clients. Marc Virgile, the owner of the vineyard, believes women have no place in wine. I doubt he'll approve of my holding the tasting. Plus he can be..." Solange paused, glancing around as if Marc de Virgile might be lurking nearby.

"Difficult?" Henri asked.

Solange grinned. "If that were the case, I could deal with it. He's impossible. Still, he and DR got along well, and I'm doing this for DR. I'll survive."

"When did you receive the email?" Henri asked.

"Seventy-two hours ago. At exactly 7:30 pm. The same time the tasting is scheduled for tonight. I was shocked when I saw it." A tear ran down Solange's face. "I can't get used to the fact the DR isn't around. He was a great friend." Solange swallowed and stared directly into Henri's eyes. "Are you private investigators?"

Henri opened his eyes wide. "Goodness, no. We're booksellers. Our stands are down on the Quai Malaquais. We're appraising DR's books."

A look of puzzlement flashed through Solange's eyes. "But I thought..."

Ava frowned. *Why would Solange believe they were private investigators?*

Solange looked embarrassed. "I'm sorry. I'd hoped Garance would do something."

"About what?" Ava asked trying to understand the woman before her.

Solange put her hands on her hips. "Why would a dead man send an email? It's suspicious, isn't it?"

Deep in thought, Henri balanced back on his heels. "The fact that it came exactly seventy-two hours before the tasting sounds like it was a pre-programmed. It didn't ask you to carry out the tasting, did it?"

Solange shook her head. "No."

Ava eyed Henri. *What was he getting at?*

"You said DR had never invited you to a tasting of Domaine de Kirjac. Maybe he wanted you here as a participant."

Solange was astonished. "As a surprise?"

"That's my guess," Henri replied.

A look of relief ran across Solange's face. "That means his death was an accident. DR's death was so stupid. It would be easier to accept if it wasn't an accident. But that would mean someone wanted to hurt him, and that's impossible.

Totally impossible."

"How did you meet him?" Ava asked.

"My thesis was on Burgundy wine. It's my specialty. David, DR, read it and contacted me," Solange replied.

Ava tilted her head sideways. "To work with him?"

Solange laughed. "No. DR was a one-man operation. He wanted to know more about wine from Burgundy in the post-war years. Many records were lost or difficult to find. I'm a *rat de bibliotheque*... a library rat who spends most of my time going through old archives. I told him what I knew, and, in exchange, he introduced me to many important people in Burgundy."

Henri raised his eyebrows, surprised. "Marc Virgile?"

Solange shook her head. "No. Not Marc Virgile."

"What are your plans now?" Henri asked.

Solange shrugged. "I'd hope to collaborate with DR on a book on Burgundy's biggest wineries. Now I'll have to do it alone."

Ava noticed that Solange hadn't mentioned the foundation. Did she know that DR hadn't mentioned her in his will?

"Or maybe it's time to write a book on another region... perhaps Bordeaux," Solange added.

Henri burst out laughing.

Solange was astonished by his reaction.

"I'm from Bordeaux. It's not a region that's open to outsiders, either," Henri replied.

An enigmatic smile crossed Solange's face. "When I want to do something, I do it. Let me show you the shop…"

Solange strolled over to the wooden shelves that the bottles were on. "As booksellers, you'll appreciate that the store sold stationary and books for over eighty years. DR bought the shop after its owner died. It came with its inventory. There are still a few crates of old school supplies in the cellar."

Henri ran his hand along the edge of a shelf. Watching him, Ava imagined generations of neighborhood children choosing their notebooks and pencils in the shop.

Ava took a bottle off the shelf. It was a 2016 California wine. A handwritten paper that had BS24 was placed under the bottle. "Are these valuable wines?"

"Not at all. I'm puzzled that he had this type of wine here." She waved her hands at the shelves. "I wouldn't drink most of this, but DR must have had his reasons. Maybe he knew the vintners who made the wine."

"How did DR go from inexpensive wines like this to Grand Crus that go for thousands of euros per bottle?" Henri asked.

Solange beamed. "That was DR. He was full of contradictions."

Henri pointed at the open bottles of Domaine de Kirjac. "Did he keep those in the shop?"

Solange shook her head. "No. The bottles were in the store when I arrived this afternoon."

"So the vineyard has the key?" Ava asked.

"There's no reason they wouldn't. DR never kept anything valuable here. The last few years, he was rarely here. He spent most of his time running around the globe. I don't know why he kept a shop except to keep in touch with his roots. Maybe make a new convert or two," Solange said. "But first the person would have to pass the DR test."

Curious, Ava tilted her head to the side. "Which was?"

Solange smiled. "DR either liked you or he didn't. There was no changing his mind once he'd made his decision."

"Was he ever wrong?" Henri asked.

A strange look appeared on Solange's face. "Sometimes. We didn't agree on everything." She checked her watch. "It seems like everyone is going to be fashionably late. Let me show you the cellar. It's amazing."

They walked to the far end of the shop. Solange opened a heavy wooden door and turned on a light. "Hold onto the wall. The steps are really steep." She grabbed a key from next to the door. "I'm always terrified the door will slam and lock me in."

As they climbed down the stone stairs, the air grew cooler and had a damp musty odor to it.

"We must be right on the edge of the *carrières de Montmartre* here," Henri said as the reached the bottom.

Ava raised her eyebrows. The Montmartre quarries were abandoned subterranean mines that were connected by galleries. They were mined for their gypsum during the Roman Gaul period, which was used to make "plaster of Paris" and the limestone that was used as a building material in the city.

Solange nodded. "We're right next to them. That's one of the reasons it's so cool here."

"It would be a good place to keep old wine," Henri said as he ran his finger over the mold on the wall.

"I don't know if I'd want to keep expensive bottles down here," Solange said. "DR loved the cellar. He often joked if Armageddon came, he'd have a place to hide."

There was a loud banging noise from above.

Henri smiled. "It appears our fellow tasters have arrived."

"The show must go on," Solange said with a sigh as she turned and hurried up the steps

Henri gazed around the cellar. He walked over to a crate, opened it and peered inside. It was full of old notebooks.

"What do you think?" Ava asked.

"We'd better hurry or we'll miss the show."

CHAPTER 7

A slim well-dressed man Asian man in his thirties wearing sunglasses, an expensive suit with a back T-shirt under it and shoes with no socks was chatting with Solange when Henri and Ava emerged from the cellar.

Hearing them approach, the man turned toward them with a candid smile. "Lee Baresi," he said, making a mock bow.

Solange presented Henri and Ava to the new arrival.

Lee pushed his thick black hair off his face and glanced around. "I'm glad to see the three of you. When I received the invitation, I wasn't entirely sure if it was a joke or not. It's not like I could text David back and expect a response."

"Where you in Paris when you got the email?" Henri asked.

"Heavens, no. I was in the Hamptons, outside of New York. I considered calling Marc Virgile to see if there really was a tasting but decided that a round trip New York-Paris would be less risky," Lee said with a wicked grin.

"Did you know David well?" Ava asked Lee.

Lee thought before speaking. "Well? Do we ever know someone well?"

Henri remained silent as he studied Lee.

Sensing they were waiting for more of a response, Lee continued, "I've worked with DR on and off over the years. When I got the invitation, I was astonished. But once invited, I'd be a fool not to come. People would die to taste Domaine de Kirjac."

Ava winced upon hearing his words. *Had someone killed to taste Marc Virgile's wines?*

"Are you in the wine world?" Lee asked. "I've never seen you at any auctions."

Ava didn't find Lee's question strange. She imagined in the rarefied world of high-end Grand Crus, the buyers were well known to each other.

Henri grinned. "Ava and I are book dealers. We're appraising DR's books. Do you have a wine shop?"

Lee shook his head. "I'm a wine intermediary who buys high-end wine for others… like DR was. We both deal with wealthy clients although DR had the upper hand because of his gift…"

Ava looked puzzled.

Solange smiled at her. "DR could taste any wine, even the most obscure wine, and remember it years later. People trusted him because of that."

Lee nodded. "It was a rare, rare gift. Few have it."

"How did you get into wine?" Ava asked, trying to find out more about the young man.

Lee chuckled. "I have expensive tastes in wine. Since I'm not part of the 1%, I find wine for people who are. I have the best of both worlds. I drink fabulous wines, and I do it on someone else's dime."

Increasingly nervous, Solange checked her watch. "When are the others coming?"

"How do you know that there are others?" Henri asked.

Flustered, Solange frowned. "I just assumed there were." She walked to the front of the store and pulled up the shade.

Lee moved toward the bottles. When he saw that the labels were covered, he smiled. "This is DR's last laugh… Seeing which of us is the best taster."

Henri whispered to him. "2003?"

Lee whispered back to Henri. "The summer was a scorcher. It was so hot that streams dried up. Some vineyards started picking as early as mid-August. Many of the wines were exceptional. Not as good as a 1976 or a 1947… but exceptional none the less." His eyes lit up. "If one of these is a 2003 Domaine de Kirjac red, my trip was worth it."

Ava counted the wine glasses that were lined up in rows There were eight wines to taste and ten rows of eight glasses. "You're expecting ten people?" Ava asked Solange who was increasingly nervous.

"A guestimate," Solange responded eyeing the door.

Lee crossed his arms. "Anyone who was invited will come. It's rare that you find wines by Domaine de Kirjac on the market. Marc Virgile has more than enough collectors who would pay any price for his wine."

Ava glanced at the wine bottles. "How much would a bottle of this wine go for?"

Instantly, Lee became the ultimate professional. "A 2003 Domaine de Kirjac would run from 1000 to 1200 euros… if you could find it. But you can't. So it's priceless."

Before Ava could ask Lee more questions about the wine, the door opened. A large, heavyset man in his early sixties clad in an impeccably cut navy blue suit entered. A shock of well-cut thick grey hair fell over his forehead. He entered the room as if he owned it.

Solange stepped forward. "Roger. How lovely to see you."

"Solange. Always a delight to see you." The man turned to Henri, Ava and Lee. "Roger Allard. Wine broker." He nodded to Lee. "Mr. Baresi… a pleasure."

Lee wasn't taken in by the man's mocking praise. "The pleasure is mine. Please call me Lee."

Ignoring Ava and Henri, Roger turned to Solange. "When are the others coming?"

"The others?" Solange asked, knitting her eyebrows together.

"People with the means to buy Domaine de Kirjac," Roger said with a toss of his head.

Ignoring the slight, Henri stepped toward Roger and held out his hand. "Henri DeAth. I'm a wine lover, but I certainly can't pretend to have your level of expertise."

Hearing the pronunciation of Henri's last name, Roger pursed his lips. He didn't know if Henri was mocking him or not. "That's an unusual last name," he said after a long pause.

"It's Flemish, but I'm from Bordeaux," Henri replied.

Roger smiled and relaxed. "You're in for a wonderful tasting. Don't get me wrong. There are some fine wines in Bordeaux. But Burgundy wines top them by far. And even by Burgundy standards, the wines of Domaine de Kirjac are exceptional. That's why I'm here on the hottest afternoon in the summer." Roger walked over to the tasting table and was surprised to see the labels covered. "A blind tasting?"

"As per Marc Virgile's instructions," Solange said.

Ava eyed Roger Allard. *What a jerk!*

Roger spun toward Ava as if he could read her thoughts. "Excuse me if I don't indulge in niceties. I'm old enough that I don't care what people think. This is the first time I've seen you at a tasting."

Ava eyes met Roger's eyes, defiant. "This is my first time at a Burgundy wine tasting."

Roger looked troubled. "DR invited you? I find that astonishing."

"Astonishing? How many times have you gotten an invitation to a tasting from beyond the grave?" a slender blonde-haired woman in her mid-forties with pale skin said as she strode across the shop.

The woman was dressed simply in a white shift dress with a coral necklace twisted around her neck. Expensive leather sandals in the same coral color were on her feet. Her attire reeked money and taste, the kind of taste that was inborn and passed down through generations.

Roger walked up to the woman and kissed her on her hand in an exaggerated gesture. "Diane! What a pleasure."

Diane smiled at everyone. "Diane de la Floch. And don't let Roger's performance fool you. We don't like each other at all."

"I adore you, Diane! I've always adored you. You know that," Roger said with an indulgent smile as if Diane were a capricious child.

With a wry smile that barely hid her dislike for the man, Diane smiled back at him.

The door opened and closed noisily.

A tall, slightly pudgy man in his mid-forties with dark brown hair hurried across the shop. He was wearing a wrinkled white linen shirt and jeans. He has sports shoes on his feet. The watch on his wrist was the price of a small car. Out of breath, the man looked at everyone there, flustered. "I hope I'm not late. I'm François Croix…"

"For those of you who don't know François, he owns a

Premier Cru winery in Burgundy," Roger explained.

Ava knew that Burgundy wine was divided into three classifications. At the top of the pyramid were the Grand Cru wines. Below that were the Premier Cru wines and village wines that bore the name of the villages that they were grown in were at the bottom.

"My wine sells just as well and is better quality than many Grand Crus," François protested.

Diane glowered at Roger. "François's wine is excellent. You know that as well as I do."

Once again, Henri took he introductions in hand. "I'm Henri DeAth, and this is Ava Sext. We're appraising DR's library."

François grinned. "Sorry. Receiving DR's mail threw me for a loop. I'm François Croix..."

Diane sighed. "François and I are cousins."

François turned to Diane to speak, but she glared at him. Ignoring Solange, he walked over to the shelves and began to look at the wine on them.

Solange introduced Diane to Henri, Ava and Lee.

Diane smiled a Lee. "You were at the Sotheby's dinner in Geneva last year after the Grand Cru auction."

Lee tilted his head to the side. "I'm honored you noticed me."

"I notice all my competitors," Diane replied. She turned

to Ava. "Wine buying has turned into a blood sport. Money isn't enough. You need knowledge and an inside track to access the best bottles. Lee Baresi has two of the three and represents impossibly deep-pocketed individuals who should be delighted with his track record."

Pleased, Lee smiled. "You also have an impeccable record for scoring impossible to buy wines, Madame de la Floch."

"Please, call me Diane. Everyone does." Diane looked around the shop and sighed. "DR's death was so tragic... so unnecessary. Still he left us this last surprise. Who else is coming?" Diane demanded swirling toward Solange.

Solange shrugged. "I don't know. DR sent out the invitations. We'll have to wait."

A look of astonishment ran across François Croix's face. "DR sent the invitations? How is that possible? He died three months ago!"

Diane eyed François as if he were an idiot. "Didn't you see who sent you the email?"

François snarled at her. "Of course, I did. I assumed the mail was sent by an assistant."

"That's the magic of software. It plans everything for us... Even after we're dead," Henri joked.

Troubled, François didn't appear convinced.

There was another knock on the door. A large red-faced man in his early seventies, dressed in jeans and a dark blue shirt entered the shop. His hands were enormous. He ignored everyone and strode directly over to the bottles. "You decanted the wine sufficiently?" he asked Solange with the air of someone who was used to having other people follow his orders.

Astonished by the man's imperious behavior, Solange answered with one word. "Yes!"

"Good." The man turned to the others. "Diane! Always lovely to see you."

Delighted to be addressed first, Diane smiled her best smile. "The pleasure is all mine, Marc."

Marc! Ava studied the man closely. This must be the infamous Marc Virgile. He didn't look like the monster everyone had described, but the evening was young.

Marc eyed François. "François. What a surprise to see you."

Hearing the way that Marc insisted on the word "surprise", François's face fell immediately.

Marc now approached Roger. "And Roger, of course. What would a tasting be without you?"

Roger had an unreadable expression on his face. "Marc! To what do we owe this honor? I've never seen you at a tasting for your wines."

Marc didn't answer. Instead, he turned to Solange, Henri and Ava. "Excuse me for ignoring you. Old friends first."

Roger didn't crack a smile upon hearing that. François

appeared ill at ease while Diane smiled graciously at Marc.

"I'm Marc Virgile, the producer of the modest wines we'll be tasting."

Henri smiled. "To meet you and taste your wines is a great honor. I'm Henri DeAth."

Suddenly, François stepped toward Henri. "I know you. You were the notary on the sale of a chateau my wife's sister bought in Bordeaux."

"I was a notary in a former life." Henri acknowledged with a smile.

François raised his eyebrows and looked at the others. "Henri was not just a notary. He was THE notary in Bordeaux. If you had an unsolvable problem, he was the notary who would solve it for you."

Intrigued, Marc eyed Henri from head to foot. "A former notary? Does that even exist? You didn't do anything nefarious to get booted out of the profession, I hope." Marc smiled at the others who appeared shocked by his words. "A French notary could kill someone in broad daylight in front of three police officers and continue on as a notary."

Henri chuckled. "I didn't kill anyone. Not yet… I just wanted another life."

Diane eyed François. "I understand completely."

François shook his head. "For those of you who don't know, not only is Diane my cousin but our families hoped we'd marry. She decided otherwise to my great regret. She got freedom..."

"And you got the winery," Diane said in a cold voice. "Our fathers owned the vineyard together. When my father died, the family chose François instead of me to run it."

"If we'd married, you'd have had the vineyard and me," François joked.

"That was a price I wasn't prepared to pay," Diane responded with a cold stare.

Roger shook his head and smiled at Diane. "Your father was pig-headed, Diane. No offense, François... But Diane has more business sense in her little finger than you have in your entire body."

Diane eyed Roger with gratitude. François opened his mouth to protest but fell silent. Watching him, Ava sensed that he often did that.

"If you're no longer a notary, what do you do now?" Marc asked Henri with true curiosity.

"Books. I buy and sell books. I have a stand down on the Quai Malaquais. Ava has a stand next to mine," Henri replied.

"How did you meet DR?" Diane asked Henri.

"We're appraising his book collection," Henri replied leaving out the part that they had never met DR.

Roger reared his head back, outraged. "I'm astonished that DR invited people who weren't wine connoisseurs."

"DR must have had his reasons," Marc replied.

The room fell silent.

Nervous, Solange stepped forward. "I'm delighted you're all here. I suggest we start."

Ava was bewildered. "Shouldn't we wait for the others?"

Marc shook his head. "It's 7:50. Obviously, there are no others."

When Solange poured wine from the first bottle into the glasses, Roger guffawed. "A blind tasting, Marc. You never cease to surprise me."

Marc smiled. "If I have my way, that will continue."

Solange passed around small notebooks. Domaine de Kirjac was embossed on them. Each person got a small gold pen, which was also embossed, with the winery's name.

"Is this some sort of test?" Diane asked Marc, keeping her eyes on him. Her expression showed that she was on guard.

"My reasons for doing so will be clear by the end of the tasting," Marc responded.

Everyone moved closer to the tasting table. Solange poured wine from each bottle into the glasses before each person. "Tonight, we're tasting eight bottles of Domaine de Kirjac. For those of you who don't know it, it's a winery in Burgundy that produces red and white Grand Cru wines. The winery has been in the same family for over 100 years. It has a very small production… only 270,000 bottles in good years. They're all sold before they're even bottled. The chateau has a mythical "cave" made up of both of its own wines and wine from other Burgundy producers."

Marc Virgile cleared his throat and began to speak. "I wish DR could be here. He was a good friend in a world where true friendship is rare. And for those of you who doubted the sincerity of our relationship, I feel sorry for you," Marc said, shooting a look at Roger. "DR and I shared an affinity for the greater truths and untruths of life. Don't get me wrong, DR listened to money but it wasn't his main motivation like it is for some."

A pall fell over the room. Ava glanced at Henri who was studying everyone's faces.

"Shall we begin?" Solange said.

Roger frowned. "There's no spit bowl?"

Marc shook his head. "You don't spit out Domaine de Kirjac."

"Of course not," François chimed in.

Diane gave him a look that seemed to say "you poor fool".

Marc lifted his glass to his nose and sniffed. The others immediately followed his example. People swirled, sniffed, studied the color, tasted and then tasted again. They then scribbled furiously in the small notebook.

Ava swirled, sniffed and tasted. As she did, she was overwhelmed by the exquisiteness of each wine. Choosing between them would be like choosing one of your children as a favorite. As she tasted, she peered around the room at the others. Solange was focused on the contents of her glass. Henri's attention was on the wine, but he had an inscrutable expression on his face. Intensely focused on the wine before them, Diane and Lee alternated tasting and writing.

At the fourth glass, Marc took a big sip and shook his head in approval.

François pursed his lips. "It's exquisite. But you can't possible expect us to guess the years for wines most of us have never tasted."

"I expect you to try," Marc replied.

As Diane tasted glass number five, a triumphant smile appeared on her face.

Lee eyed her. "May the best person win."

"Only if it's me," Diane said and moved on to glass number six.

Roger put his glass number eight down and spoke out loud as he wrote. "Creamy elegance.... silky raspberry and cherry fruit with a long finish. It's a jewel, Marc. Definitely, a 1997."

Marc didn't react.

"I agree, a 1997," Lee said sipping wine number eight.

Diane shook her head. "In 1995, Marc's father died. 1996 was Marc's first year making wine. This is a 1996."

"Bravo, Diane," Marc said. "Wine owes as much to

family politics as it does to *terroir*."

Ava listened with interest. Terroir was a French term, which referred to the geology, geography, climate and other factors that gave each vineyard's wines their specific qualities.

François tasted wine number seven and gave a running commentary on his thoughts. "Gingerbread spice, slightly astringent with medium body."

"Poppycock!" Marc said shaking his head. "You might as well have said "Star Wars meets Godzilla". I don't taste a bit of gingerbread spice."

Humiliated, François fell silent.

Tasting the eighth glass of wine, the phrase "nectar from the Gods" ran through Ava's mind. Eyeing Marc Virgile, she wondered which God he would be: Zeus with his lightning bolts trying to bring order to his ruling family or Ares, the God of War.

Seeing Ava's troubled expression, Diane smiled at her. "Marc is just joking. He's fishing for compliments. His wines are sublime. All of the wines we tasted tonight are exceptional. But the last glass is beyond that."

'What vintage?" Marc de Virgile asked her with a twinkled in his eye.

Diane didn't hesitate. "2001."

Roger shook his head. "I'd go for a 2003!"

François remained silent and scribbled in his notebook. He didn't offer a guess as to the year.

Lee tasted the wine again. "I agree with Diane. 2001. The wine is classic but pure and expressive."

Marc Virgile turned to Solange. "Show them the label."

Solange took the cover off the label. It was a 2001.

Diane clapped her hands together in delight.

Marc Virgile turned to Lee and Diane. "Very good. And the rest?"

Solange took the covers off the labels. Diane had 5 out of the 8 right. Lee had 4. Roger had 6. François had 3 out of 8. Solange didn't reveal her evaluations and no one asked her for them. She was a non-entity for the people there.

Marc eyed everyone around the table. "I'm impressed. But you don't get the prize yet…"

Roger frowned.. "Yet? What do you mean, Marc?"

Diane pursed her lips. "Marc means that there is something behind this little tasting."

"You're a wise woman, Diane," Marc said. "This tasting was DR's idea. He also chose the people to invite. What's behind this is that I have decided to sell off some old bottles from my cave… a last sale. After that, I'll be turning over the reins to my nephew."

"Is Sotheby's selling your wine?" Roger asked, suddenly all business.

"It will be a private sale. I want to sell the wine to someone who will appreciate it and keep it for a few years,"

Marc Virgile said. "I don't want flippers or billionaires who will guzzle down my wine in strip clubs. DR chose each of you for various reasons. One… you all have the means to buy the wine or know people who do. Two… you're discreet. I don't want my nephew to learn about the sale. Don't get me wrong. It's my wine to do with as I please. Even when my nephew takes over, he won't get my shares until I die."

Clearly disturbed, Henri listened to Marc Virgile speak.

"If it's money, I'll top any price," Roger Allard said.

Marc shook his head. "Yes, money is important. I'd be lying if I said it wasn't. But this is my last sale. Bottles that have been in my cave for ages will be leaving. Some of them are bottles that you didn't even know still existed," Marc said.

Lee fixed his gaze on Marc as his mind ran over what those bottles might be. "A Romanée-Conti 1975?"

"Perhaps" Marc Virgile replied with an enigmatic smile.

There was an immediate buzzing in the room. Although no one spoke, you could feel the excitement growing.

"How will you choose the buyer," François asked.

"I'm holding an early dinner this Saturday. A friend has very generously lent me his hotel particulier not far from here. We'll eat. We'll talk and taste wine, and then I'll make my choice," Marc replied.

"So it will be the four of us… Diane, Lee, François and myself," Roger asked.

"I'm inviting everyone here to the dinner and the

tasting," Marc said.

Roger frowned. He wasn't happy at all with this.

Henri smiled. "It will be an honor to participate."

Marc smiled strangely at Henri. "Your advice might come in useful."

Solange stared at Marc but didn't speak.

"So it's a popularity contest?" Roger asked.

"Much more than that... I'm choosing a home for my wine," Marc protested. "Now let's help Solange tidy up."

Everyone brought their glasses over to the table with the glasses. Lee picked up a wine bottle and studied the label. "Domaine de Kirjac's label has changed over the years."

"Up until fifteen years ago, everything was very artisanal. Sometimes we had two different labels for the same wine. Those days are gone," Marc Virgile said, nostalgic. "Perhaps it's good that I'm moving on. My nephew is more in touch with the times."

"Do you need us to help you wash up?" Ava asked Solange.

Solange shook her head. "I'll do it tomorrow."

Ava grabbed her tasting notebook off the corner of the table where she had left it and joined Henri who was chatting with Marc.

"Thank you for inviting me," Ava said.

"How did you find the tasting?" Marc asked her.

Ava grinned. "Fascinating and life-changing!"

Marc smiled at her. "I predict that Saturday will be even more life-changing. Although perhaps not as some would like."

Roger moved to the door. "I'll see you all on Saturday."

Marc raised his hands in the air. "Before you leave, one last remark. Before he died, DR believed someone here was trying to kill him."

Diane clutched her neck. "That's a terrible joke, Marc."

"I'm not joking. He thought one of you wanted to kill him," Marc replied. "Does anyone want to confess?"

"That's not funny," François snapped.

Marc shook his head. "I don't intend it to be funny. DR had intended to hold the tasting to smoke the person out. It's too late for that now."

Henri stared at Marc. "In my experience as a notary, it's never good to take justice into your own hands."

Marc took a deep breath. "I don't care about justice. I just care about finding a good home for my wine. If someone here did have a hand in DR's fall, that is between them and divine justice. DR is dead. There's no bringing him back." He paused. "I'll send you an email with the details on Saturday morning."

Silent, people filed out. No one spoke. Marc sauntered

off and vanished around the corner. Roger disappeared down the street. Only Solange, Henri and Ava were left in the store.

"Do you think Marc was joking?" Solange asked, worried.

"I'm sure he is. I can't imagine anyone holding a tasting to find their killer," Henri said.

Ava was silent. DR wasn't just anyone. He was someone who had held a tasting from beyond the grave.

CHAPTER 8

Each step took them further and further away from DR's wine shop and into a quieter, more residential section of Montmartre. Neither Ava not Henri had said a word since leaving the tasting.

Feeling her stomach grumble, Ava stopped in front of a crepe shop, the only restaurant that was open. She hovered in front of the door. It was totally empty which was never a good sign. "What do you think?"

Henri shook his head. "I'll pass. I intend to go home, sit in the garden, contemplate my tomatoes and mull over what just happened," Henri said. "What's your view on the tasting?"

"Something beyond strange is going on. But what? Money or love?" Ava asked, referencing Henri's belief that every crime in France is based on love or money. But then wasn't that true everywhere?

"Definitely money. But money can buy many things… It's our job to discover what each one there really wants," Henri said. "Including Marc Virgile…"

As the taxi neared Ava's apartment, she could feel her stomach growl again. "You're sure you don't want to eat something, Henri?"

Henri shook his head. "I prefer to have an early night. We can have lunch at Café Zola and plan our next move."

"You're right as usual. *La nuit porte conseil,*" Ava replied.

When the taxi pulled up in front of her building, Ava kissed Henri on the cheeks goodbye and climbed out. By tomorrow, they both would have had time to reflect on what they had experienced, and their analysis of the situation and the players would be sharper. Besides, skipping dinner had never killed anyone…

Walking up the stairs to her apartment, Ava ran over the people she had met at the tasting. Each one could have come directly from central casting for a film on wine making…

Marc Virgile, the wine maker, was a caricature of a headstrong wine maker who didn't care what people thought. His wines gave him power over people who were wealthier than he was.

Lee Baresi had an easy breeziness that went with a privileged background but the streetwise intelligence of someone who had to navigate his way through a business where competition was fierce, and he was an outsider. He had been charmingly polite to everyone at the tasting, but Ava sensed that he didn't believe the role he was playing for a second. In fact, several times Ava had caught a glint in his eye that said it was all a performance.

Roger Allard was used to having his own way and making people jump when he wanted them to. But even he had to bow down in front of Marc Virgile, something that he clearly disliked doing. In fact, he hated it. Ava wondered what Roger Allard's relationship with DR had been over the years.

Then there was Diane de la Floch and François Croix. It was impossible to believe that they were destined to be married. François was no match for Diane. While the two weren't friends, Ava wondered if they would join forces if need be. Was blood thicker than money?

The biggest mystery was that all five had come to a hastily improvised tasting in the middle of August. When had Marc Virgile discovered that the DR had scheduled the tasting before he had died? And if DR had set his computer to send off the invitations automatically, then why send them off only seventy-two hours in advance?

Solange Vitrang was also a mystery. Part of Ava hoped they could become friends. Solange was intelligent, didn't take herself too seriously, worked hard in her field, and had a sense of humor. However, there was something bubbling under the surface that Ava couldn't put her finger on. Maybe dealing with people like Roger Allard who had treated her like a lowly employee, barely tolerating her presence, had gotten to her. François Croix hadn't even spoken to her. The patriarchy was alive and well in Burgundy.

Ava smiled as she remembered the looks on the men's faces when Marc Virgile had invited Henri, Ava and Solange to his dinner. Lee Baresi had been the only one who hadn't appeared to care one way or the other.

Hearing her stomach growl again, Ava craved a duck or meat dish, even though it was too hot for that. She debated walking back down the steps and picking up Lebanese takeout from a nearby caterer but decided against it. She would rustle up something to eat at home. Although given her kitchen was as poorly stocked as DR's, she wondered just what that meal might consist of.

As she continued up the stairs, music wafted down from an upper floor. Ava was surprised. As far as she knew, she was the only one in the building. Even the *concierge*, the guardian, had gone on holiday. Perhaps someone had lent their apartment to a friend. When she reached the fifth floor, she could hear the music clearly enough to identify the band: Creedence Clearwater Revival.

Ava let go of the railing and sprinted up the remaining stairs to the top floor.

Creedence Clearwater Revival was Nate's favorite group.

The music could mean only one thing -- Nate was there!

When she reached the door to her apartment, a single red rose was taped to it. Grabbing the rose, she flung the door open.

Standing over the stove, Nate looked up. "I was wondering when you'd get back."

Ava wrapped her arms around him and kissed him. "Why didn't you tell me you were coming to Paris?"

Nate kissed her back and continued cooking. "I tried. But when you didn't answer your phone, I decided to surprise you."

Suddenly, Ava understood why Henri hadn't felt like going out to dinner. He knew that Nate was there. "You spoke with Henri?"

"That's why we're having tuna with Asian sauce. Henri said you had chicken for lunch and were going to a wine tasting for Burgundy Grand Crus so I chose tonight's menu based on that. We're also having a lamb's lettuce salad with Italian goat cheese and late summer cherries for dessert."

"What if I had gone out dancing till dawn?" Ava teased.

"I would have eaten alone, but I would have drunk like a king," Nate said pointing to a bottle of wine on the counter. "A simple Burgundy from Marsannay… nothing like what you drank this evening, but it will do."

Ava picked up the wine bottle. The wine was two years old. She poured herself a glass and tasted it. She looked up to see Nate watching her.

"Does it meet your approval?"

"It's "Mick Jagger meets Damien Hirst"…" Ava announced with a grin.

Nate shook his head. "That's your new found wine tasting vocabulary?"

"If you'd been there, you'd understand," Ava said as she poured Nate some wine.

Nate swirled his wine and tasted it. "A complex intense nose of blackberry and liquorice. Elegant with a hint of mocha!"

Astonished, Ava tasted the wine again. "You tasted all that?"

Nate chuckled. "I looked it up on the wine site."

"That's cheating," Ava protested. "Now tell me why you're here?"

"With you or in Paris," Nate asked with a grin.

Ava's lips parted in a smile. "Don't be silly. In Paris."

"We had a meeting with the French and English co producers today. The Italian producer couldn't come so he sent me."

"How long will you be here for?"

Nate kissed her neck. "Long enough."

Ava raised her eyebrows. "Tomorrow?"

Nate sighed. "I have a 7 a.m. flight to Rome. What are you and Henri up to besides a tasting?"

"He told you about the case?"

"No. But after I called him, I remembered you said he had a wedding in Bordeaux. Since he's in Paris, I assumed something is up."

Ava leaned against the counter. "We're not sure what's going on. We'll only discover that on Saturday. But we drank heavenly wine with the oddest people."

Nate served the food directly onto their plates and carried them over to the table. Ava followed with the wine and the wine glasses.

"You choose the music for dinner," Nate told her.

Ava walked over to the record player and went through the albums. Ava had inherited the apartment from her late uncle. All the furniture and his vintage record collection from the sixties had come with it. There were hundreds of albums. Ava slowly made her way through them. She pulled out a record by Fleetwood Mac. She put it on the turntable and grinned when she saw the dedication on the album cover: *To Charlie, the best roadie ever.* Her late uncle, a former New Scotland Yard detective, had been a rock band roadie in his youth.

"Being a roadie in the sixties must have been a blast!" Ava said to Nate, almost envious.

"Are you thinking of changing professions?"

As the music started to play, Ava walked over and kissed him on top of his head. "You're lucky that I only half-listen to what you say."

Nate sat back in his chair and sipped his wine. "Since when have you started tasting Grand Crus that cost hundreds of euros?"

"Since I met Garance Pons, Henri's friend, who asked him for help"

"You haven't found a dead body, have you?"

Ava bristled with annoyance. "Of course not. Why would you ask that?"

"As I remember, that's how we met…" Nate said, referring to the jewel thief who was murdered on the film set where Nate and Ava had first laid eyes on each other. Nate took a bite of his tuna. "Exquisite.! Even if I do say so myself."

Ava bit into her tuna. It was amazing although she had no intention of telling Nate that. He considered himself the Cordon Bleu in their relationship. He once joked that the only thing she had in her refrigerator when they started dating was face cream.

"You're sure there was no body?" Nate probed.

"Are you going to let me tell the story, or are you going to keep jumping in?" Ava asked.

Nate grinned. "Please speak..."

"Thank you." Ava leaned over and squeezed his hand lovingly. "Before we start, what is your favorite quality in a woman?"

Nate frowned. "A woman or you?"

"Both." Ava tilted her head to the side, puzzled. "Aren't they the same?"

"In both men and women, I like people who are straight forward and do what they say they will do. You have that in spades. In addition, I like your whimsy."

Ava wasn't sure what to make of that. "Whimsy?"

Nate nodded. "You take an ordinary situation and make it special."

"What about my intelligence, wit, get up and go and incredible sexiness?" Ava asked.

"That goes without saying. Now tell me what happened."

Ava took another bite of the tuna. She really needed to learn how to cook. "Henri's friend, Garance, is a notary. She asked him to appraise the books of a wine broker."

"In the middle of August… just like that?"

"Just like that."

Nate's dubious expression made it clear he found the story odd. "Just like the wine tasting this evening?"

Ava nodded. "Yes."

"Henri said you were going to taste Grand Cru wines. Why do that in the middle of August? Why not wait until the rentrée?"

"What if I were to tell you a dead man invited everyone three days ago?" Ava asked.

Nate took the bottle and poured them each more wine. "I'd say that's a tale worth hearing."

As they ate, Ava told him about David Rose and the invitation to the tasting.

Nate clicked his tongue. "It sounds like a film. I don't

believe David, or DR as you called him, sent the invitation."

"Why not?" Ava asked.

Nate tapped the side of his nose with his forefinger. "Intuition."

"I agree." Ava took a bite of the lamb's lettuce salad. "There's nut oil on it!"

"There is," Nate affirmed.

"But I don't have nut oil in my pantry," Ava protested.

"You didn't have any milk, olive oil, or butter either. I went shopping."

Ava sighed. "DR's kitchen is better stocked than mine, and he's dead."

Nate burst out laughing. "I don't see the connection. Tell me about Garance, the notary. A love interest for Henri?"

Ava's eyes lit up. "Impossible to know. If there was a spark, it took place a long time ago. They have a warm relationship for people who haven't seen each other in a while. So yes, maybe an old flame," Ava said. "She's gorgeous and funny."

"Whimsical?" Nate asked with a grin.

"I don't know her that well," Ava replied.

"Why didn't she go to the tasting?"

"She's off to Singapore… following the money," Ava replied as she brushed his arm with her fingers. "Do you really have to leave tomorrow?"

"Normally, I should have left this evening."

Ava sighed. "I'm not complaining. There's something going on, and Henri and I have to discover what that is."

"And romance cuts into your sleuthing time?" Nate asked in false outrage.

"Something like that. Plus, there are thousands of books to catalog. That right there will be time consuming," Ava said with a sigh as she remembered just how much work it was to organize her stand.

"DR had an accident and died… What do you think?"

Ava fell silent before speaking. "The steps are worn. It was raining, and it was dark. Maybe he'd had too much to drink. But even sober, it would have been easy to slip."

"What did the police rule?"

"An accident… They had no reason to think otherwise."

"But?" Nate asked as he removed the dinner dishes and brought over the goat's cheese and cherries.

"How do you know there is a "but"?"

"I can see it in your eyes…" Nate leaned over and kissed her forehead.

Ava shivered. Nate had an unsettling effect on her. Maybe seeing him now and then was better than seeing him all the time. It kept the magic in their relationship alive... very alive.

"What wines did you taste?" Nate asked.

In response, Ava grabbed her handbag. She removed the tasting notebook and put it on the table.

Nate pushed the notebook away. "Way too detailed for me. I'm no expert in wine. Just give me a brief overview. Besides, we have a busy evening ahead of us."

"Briefly? They were all insanely expensive rare wines produced by a wine maker from Burgundy, Marc Virgile. His family has produced wine for over 100 years. He's someone who doesn't tolerate fools lightly. In his eyes, I have no doubt that I, and over 99% of the population of France, fall into that category."

Nate swirled the wine in his glass. "And Henri?"

Ava looked amused. "He and Marc got along like a house on fire."

Nate laughed. "*Sacré* Henri!"

"Are you going to let me get back to my story or not?" Ava asked as she popped a cherry in her mouth. It had a sour sweetness that complimented the tartness of the goat's cheese.

Nate fell silent.

"Marc Virgile has decided to sell off rare bottles from the winery's cellars to the participants at the tasting. To be more specific, he's selling the wine to one of the participants. He's going to have a dinner on Saturday and choose that person."

Nate frowned. "That doesn't sound like a good idea…"

"It's a terrible idea. Henri and I are invited to the dinner. Marc Virgile also invited Solange Vitrang, the person who ran the tasting. She's a friend of DR's and an expert on the history of Burgundy wines."

"Is she in the running to buy the bottles?" Nate asked, setting his wine glass down.

"She doesn't have the means. We're talking about a lot of money," Ava replied. "I wonder why Marc Virgile isn't selling the wine directly through Sotheby's or another auction house?"

"I can think of three reasons off the top of my head: One -- taxes. Two -- discretion. And three, he doesn't have to pay a commission."

"Or maybe a mix of the three. Marc also said that DR believed that one of the people at the tasting was trying to kill him."

Nate nearly choked. "What? You're kidding?"

"Unfortunately, I'm not."

Nate swallowed before he spoke. "How did people react?"

"Like it was a bad joke," Ava said. "I don't think it was…"

Nate was silent.

"Besides Marc and Solange, there were four others there.

The first two were Diane de la Floch and François Croix. They're cousins who were destined to be married. They didn't marry. Her choice. He got the family winery. She's angry over that. A younger man was there: Lee Baresi. He's Asian but lives in New York. He clearly comes from family money, but not "throw it away on expensive wine" type of money… Charming. He buys for wealthy buyers. He was surprised by the invitation. Roger Allard, an important broker from Burgundy was also there. He's arrogant. He and Marc don't like each other."

Nate took another sip of wine. "So everyone except Solange had money or represents money. They all know one another in various ways, and are now rivals for the wine. How did Henri introduce himself?"

Ava raised her eyebrows. "You mean his profession? As a bookseller… But François Croix recognized him. Now everyone knows he was a notary."

"Bordeaux is small. That doesn't surprise me. When people talk about "'*tout Paris*" – the Parisian smart set -- they're talking about a very small pool of people."

Ava looked annoyed. "What are the rest of us? Extras?"

Nate nodded. "To the "*tout Paris*," we're probably less than extras. Tell me about Solange."

"Early thirties. She wrote her doctorate on the history of the Burgundy wine region. DR contacted her about her thesis and they became friends. Garance said that DR intended for her to have a role in his foundation. Strangely, it wasn't mentioned in his will."

"Does Solange know about this?"

"I don't know. We didn't have time to talk. She seems like my type of person though."

"Whimsical?" Nate asked.

"I can't say. She's clearly intelligent, funny and patient," Ava ventured.

Nate burst out laughing. "Patient… You?"

Ava pursed her lips in annoyance. "I can be patient. For example, I didn't respond when you just said that."

"Probably because I'm incredibly seductive," Nate said as he poured the last of the wine in their glasses.

"Incredibly over-confident is more like it."

Nate held in a smile.

"I forgot the nephew. Marc Virgile's nephew who will be taking over the winery. Marc doesn't want him to know about the sale."

"Odd. From what you tell me, Marc isn't the type to turn over the reins to someone else. Did you meet the nephew?"

Ava shook her head. "No."

"This upcoming dinner sounds like an episode of *The Hunger Games*. Everyone will compete, and Marc will name the winner."

"There are also secret rules. Marc wants the wine to go to the right person," Ava explained.

"Who might be a murderer!" Nate exclaimed.

"Or not…" Ava replied, playing the devil's advocate. "That's what Henri and I have to discover."

"I'm glad I'll be in Rome working on a film."

Ava grinned. "Out of sight. Out of mind."

Nate burst out laughing. "Nothing like knowing you're appreciated." He stood up and took Ava's hand. "It's time for some star-gazing."

As Ava followed Nate up the stairs to the tower room, she smiled. *L'amour* and a case… Things were looking up.

CHAPTER 9

The sun was high in the sky. Ava pulled the brim of her straw hat low over her forehead and strode through the vineyard. Long rows of dark green vines with purple grapes stretched out in front of her as far as the eye could see. Unable to resist, she stopped, picked a ripe grape, popped it in her mouth and bit down. It was tart, yet sweet at the same time. Looking up, she saw Marc Virgile walking toward her. He had a somber look on his face.

"You shouldn't have done that. You don't know what you've unleashed," Marc said when he reached her.

There was a low rumbling noise in the distance that began to grow louder and louder.

Marc's expression darkened. "It's too late now."

Bewildered, Ava spun around, trying to discover the source of the noise. When she turned back, Marc Virgile had vanished. In his place, a wall of red wine as high as a five-story building was racing toward her. Terrified, Ava turned on her heels and ran for her life.

Too late!

The wine slammed into her. Its raging force threw her body in the air and dragged it beneath the surface. Suffocating in the dark red liquid, Ava forced herself to the surface and gazed around. Everything was gone except for an unending sea of wine…

Startled, Ava sat up. She opened her eyes and blinked at the bright sunlight streaming through the window overhead. The wine was gone. So was the vineyard.

Ava sighed. *If you had to die, drowning in a sea of Grand Cru wine would be the way to go.*

Noticing the indent in the pillow next to her, she looked around the apartment. "Nate!" She checked the time. Nate's flight for Rome had already taken off.

She jumped out of bed, slipped her feet into her Moroccan leather slippers and moseyed toward the kitchen, stopping to choose an album. *Let it Bleed* by the Rolling Stones seemed just the thing. Hadn't Mick Jagger owned a vineyard in France?

As the first notes of "Gimme Shelter" rang out through the apartment, Ava picked up Nate's rose that was in a vase in the center of the table and smelled it. The rose had a rich earthy odor to it.

She made herself a coffee using her battered Italian espresso pot and brought the cup over to the table and tasted it.

What could be better than coffee for breakfast? Except maybe a Grand Cru wine for dinner…

Worrying that she was developing a taste for the high life, she leaned back in her chair. Something brushed against her ankles. Startled, she looked down. Mercury was staring up at her with his slanted green eyes.

Ava crouched down next to the cat. "I thought you'd gone on vacation."

Mercury swung his tail to tell her he wanted his breakfast.

Ava didn't know what the cat's name really was. She called him Mercury. Like the planet, he appeared most mornings. Mercury was well fed and well groomed. His coat was shiny. For some reason, the cat had decided that it was her job to give him breakfast. For all she knew, her place just might be one stop on his breakfast tour of the neighborhood.

Happy to see him, she took the cat food out of the cupboard , poured it in his bowl and smiled at the small animal. Having breakfast with Mercury was even better than drinking Grand Cru wines.

Ava eyed the cat but didn't pet him as he was not an affectionate cat, but then Ava wasn't an animal lover so they got along fine.

"If you could bring me a croissant every morning, you'd be perfect," Ava told him.

As usual, Mercury ignored her and continued eating.

CHAPTER 10

It was another perfect summer day in Paris. The sky was blue. There was a bright yellow sun overhead, and a gentle breeze was blowing up the rue des Saints-Pères from the Seine. Walking quickly, Ava barely noticed the weather. For her, the endless summer days were over. Time had sped up. By Saturday evening, she and Henri had to discover what was going on.

Passing by Café Zola, she peered inside and debated having another coffee. Gerard, the grumpy co-owner, dressed in the traditional waiter's uniform of a long sleeved white shirt, black trousers and a white apron tied around his waist was placing hard-boiled eggs in a metal egg holder with his back to her. Ava turned to leave.

"I can see you, Ava," Gerard shouted.

Ava stopped, puzzled. "Do you have eyes in the back of your head?"

Gerard placed the egg holder on the bar's zinc countertop. "I do actually. But even if I didn't. I could see your reflection in the mirror on the wall. Some sleuth you are. A coffee?"

Ava ignored his teasing. Gerard was one of her favorite people in Paris along with his cousin, Alain, who was the café's chef. She corrected herself instantly. Alain was more than a chef. He was a culinary wizard. "No, thank. I'm running late!"

Gerard guffawed.

Ava stared at him. "What's so funny?"

"It's not like you keep banker's hours. You were gone all afternoon yesterday," Gerard said.

"That's because I had pressing professional obligations," Ava responded.

'In August?" Gerard asked, incredulous.

Ava gave him an enigmatic smile, a smile that that she knew would drive the overly inquisitive Gerard into high gear until he learned what she had been up to.

She glanced at the chalkboard where lunch specials were posted. It was still empty. Rather than ask Gerard, she left with a breezy wave of her hand. She and Henri would discover what the specials were when they had lunch later to work on the case.

Ava liked surprises, especially culinary ones. Nate's dinner fell into that category.

Thinking of Nate, Ava smiled and crossed the street to her stand.

Most of the bookstands on the Quai Malaquais were already open. Henri's stand and hers were the exceptions. She gazed over at her fellow bookseller, Ali Beltran. He was deep in discussion with a customer who was paging through a stack of coffee table art books.

Noticing Ava, Ali raised his hand and then plunged back into his discussion.

Ava unlocked the locks on her boxes, one by one. It was a simple act that never failed to thrill her. She gazed out at the Louvre across the way, the Seine below and Notre Dame further up the river and pinched herself.

How was it possible to work in such a beautiful place?

She removed her green and white lawn chair from one of her boxes and set it up in the shade of the tree.

Ava eyed Henri's shuttered stand. By now, Henri had amassed a wealth of information about the people present at last night's tasting. His past life as a notary meant that he had an enormous network of people all over France who knew where the bodies were buried. And because Henri was Henri, they were all willing to help him… even in August. While she didn't have the contacts Henri had, Ava felt that she brought a certain Anglo-Saxon down-to-earth approach to their cases.

After all, murder was murder whether it was in Paris, the UK or Hong Kong. The dead stayed dead, and murderers tried to hide their deeds.

As for Henri's theory that French people killed for love or money, Ava guessed that it was the same in the UK. However, in France, riches were hidden. You didn't see many Rolls Royces, Lamborghinis or Ferraris roaring through the

Parisian streets. Just like it would be impossible to guess that a spectacular apartment like DR's was hidden inside such an ordinary building.

Ava pulled out her sales notebook to see how many books Ali had sold for her yesterday thanks to her new system of organization. She opened it.

Only one sale was marked in the notebook.

One.

That was impossible. Yesterday was a beautiful day. People had been out in throngs.

Frowning, Ava stared at her stand. Her fiction books were still in alphabetical order though a Becket had moved to the D's. In the non-fiction section, a *Guide to Paris* had found its way to the food section. Since the guide did have a restaurant section, she supposed that was OK.

"How was lunch?" Ali asked striding up next to her with a grin.

Ava eyed the customer who was leaving with a large stack of books under his arm. "He bought all those books?"

Ali nodded. "Why wouldn't he?"

"I only sold one book yesterday afternoon?"

"Yes," Ali replied and looked away.

Ava stared at her books again. Suddenly, her eyes lit up.

The problem was obvious.

So obvious, she should have seen it yesterday.

She turned to Ali and crossed her arms. "Why didn't you tell me?"

"If I had told you would you have listened? There are some things you have to learn for yourself. What's your conclusion?"

Ava waved her hand at her books. "People come here to find a hidden treasure. My organization takes all the fun out of finding that treasure."

"Do you need help?" Ali asked.

Ava nodded. "Ready. Set. Go."

Ali grabbed a few books and handed them to Ava. Closing her eyes, she stuck them in her stand at random. Opening her eyes, she plucked two books out and handed them to Ali who closed his eyes and did the same thing.

This back and forth went on for the next twenty minutes to the amusement of people walking past. Books went back and forth until Ava's stand was a mess.

Eyeing the chaos, Ava grinned. "Things are back to normal!"

"Lunch yesterday?" Ali asked again.

"It seems so long ago." Ava ran over lunch with Garance, DR's tragic death and some basic facts on the tasting. When she finished, Ali's eyes were wide open.

"That's incredible. What does Henri think?"

Ava leaned against her stand. "That something is wrong. We need to find out what that is."

"If you and Henri are on the case, it means DR's death was a murder!" Ali announced without the slightest bit of doubt in his voice.

Ava was startled by his reaction. "What?"

"If Miss Marple stumbles upon a dead person in an Agatha Christie book, you can be sure that that person didn't die of natural causes. It's the same with you and Henri. I don't know if it's you or Henri. Maybe it's the two of you together. But you attract murder."

Ava beamed. "Thank you. That's a really nice thing to say."

Now it was Ali's turn to look at Ava, astonished.

Ava burst out laughing. "I'm joking. But to be a sleuth, you have to have something to investigate. Henri and I have the knack of finding cases."

Ali crossed his arms. "Tell me more about the tasting."

"We drank spectacular wines," Ava acknowledged. "Domaine de Kirjac."

Ali whistled. "How was it?"

Ava shook her head. "Fabulous, I imagine. But I was so intent on discovering what was going on that I didn't pay as much attention to the wine as I should have."

"What does Nate think about the situation?" Ali asked.

Ava raised her eyebrows, bewildered. "Nate? He called you, too?"

"When you didn't answer your phone, he called to find out where you were," Ali confessed.

"And you told him I was with Henri. Why am I always the last one to know?"

"Maybe because you don't bring your cell phone with you?" Ali ventured.

Ava patted her pocket to confirm that her cell phone was with her.

Suddenly, Ali looked up. "What did Diane with the aristocratic last name look like?"

"Elegant. Well-dressed," Ava responded.

"In her forties, blond, incredibly thin with perfect skin?"

Ava raised her eyebrows. "How did you know that?"

"Because she came by earlier and asked where your stand was. And if I'm not mistaken, she's heading straight toward us."

Startled, Ava raised her eyes. Diane de la Floch was indeed approaching them. She walked like a woman on a mission.

"I'll be at my stand if you need me," Ali said. He scurried off before Ava could respond.

Ava pretended not to see Diane. But Diane wasn't

having it.

"Good morning, Ava," Diane said as she walked up to her.

Today, Diane was dressed in jeans and an immaculate white shirt. She had three gold rings on her finger set with gemstones. Ava imagined that they'd been handmade by some jeweler in Capri while Diane lingered on a nearby yacht in the Tyrrhenian Sea.

"Can we talk?" Diane asked.

Ava nodded. It was not a question.

Before speaking, Diane eyed Ava from head to foot and then looked at the stand. "Have you been running this long?"

Ava shook her head. "My uncle ran it until last year. I took over from him." Ava had no intention of telling Diane more than that.

Diane nodded. "I'll come straight to the point and lay my cards on the table. I'm sure you know that I didn't come to buy books."

Ava was equally as blunt. "Why did you come?"

Diane looked at Ava. For an instant, a look of vulnerability flashed across her face. Then her steely regard reappeared. "I came because I want to win."

Ava was puzzled. "Win what?"

"The auction. I want Marc Virgile sell me the wine," Diane stated.

"How could I possibly help?" Ava asked.

"You're a woman. We women have to stick together. Did you see how terrible Marc and Roger treated poor Solange last night? I would have said something, but it wouldn't have changed anything. And it might have gone against me in the end."

Ava shook her head. "I only met Marc Virgile yesterday. I doubt my opinion is important to him."

"For some reason, Marc likes you and Henri. The proof -- he invited you," Diane said.

"He also invited Solange. Why not ask her?"

Diane sighed. "That's a long story. When she was writing her book, she wrote that François had revolutionized the vineyard after my father's death. That's a lie. The change had started years before. My father and I did it together. François hasn't had an original idea in his life."

"Did you know your father was going to give the winery to François?" Ava asked, trying to imagine what a betrayal like that would do to someone.

"My father died unexpectedly. If he'd had more time, he would have convinced the other members of the family to name me in his place. The vineyard belongs to the extended family. The ideal situation for everyone was that François and I marry. Well, we're not in the 18th century anymore. That idea was out of the question. I married someone else. You might say I married well, and I divorced even better. The family now regrets putting François in charge. But they're stuck with him."

"Why?" Ava asked.

"To replace François, they need my vote. The only person I'll vote for is me. So they can watch the vineyard lose its glory. I won't lift a finger," Diane said with a bitter smile. "That's why buying Marc's wine is important. I'm drawing a line in the sand. For myself... For the family vineyard.... I intend to win Marc's "beauty contest". For the life of me, I can't imagine why DR invited François to the tasting."

"What do you want me to do?" Ava asked, more and more confused.

"Help me if you can. You'll only know if that's possible the night of the dinner. Marc is up to something, although I don't know what it is."

Ava stared at Diane. It was time to ask her the question that had been bothering Ava. "Do you think DR really said that one of you were out to kill him?"

Diane burst out laughing. "We're all killers in our own way. But the notion that one of us killed DR is absurd. That's classic Marc Virgile. He's troubling the waters."

"What if I can't help you?" Ava asked.

"Then don't help the others," Diane replied. "I have money. Let me know your price. This stand can't be that lucrative."

Ava was silent. She didn't know what to say.

Diane shifted to weight to her back foot. "Think about

it. The others will be trying to do the same thing. By now, Roger and François have called their friends in Bordeaux and are working their way to Henri."

"And Lee?" Ava asked.

"He's not one of us," Diane said.

Ava looked shocked.

Diane shook her head. "Not because he's Asian. It's that he's not from Burgundy. I don't know much about Lee except that we've bid for the same wines at auction, and he can be a formidable opponent. But in dealing with Marc Virgile, knowing how people from Burgundy think will be essential."

Sensing Diane was about to leave, Ava spoke, "Tell me about David Rose."

"David?" Diane pursed her lip in thought. "David was incredibly lucky. He found bottles that people would kill to buy. Maybe they did."

"You think he was killed?" Ava asked.

Diane shook her head. "I'm speaking metaphorically. Wine collectors are incredibly obsessive. If we want a certain rare wine, we'll do anything to get it. DR was an intermediary for people who wanted to remain anonymous. That must have put him under tremendous pressure. But then DR was not one to buckle under pressure… on the contrary."

"What about Solange and DR?" Ava asked, trying to understand the relationship between the two.

Diane shrugged. "I never saw them together. I don't know. She hitched her star to DR. Why? DR didn't like women -- not sexually at least. A meeting of the minds? Maybe. Maybe not… He helped her get a foot in Burgundy. That might be all there is to it." Diane waved at a black Mercedes that drove up and stopped on the other side of the street. "My driver is here. Think about my offer. You can tell me on Saturday." Diane crossed the street and slid into the back seat of the Mercedes. The Mercedes drove off.

Instantly, Ali raced over. "What did she want?"

Ava shrugged. "To bribe me."

Ali grinned. "I hope you said yes…"

Before Ava could speak, she heard the beeping of a text message on her cell phone. Sure it was from Nate, she took out her phone and read it.

The blood drained from her face.

Shaking, she turned to Ali. "Watch my stand. I have to go."

Bewildered, Ali grabbed her arm. "What is it?"

"Henri's at a clinic. There's been an accident."

CHAPTER 11

Gripping the handlebars of the bright yellow rental bike, Ava pedaled furiously up the rue de Seine toward the metro station Odeon. Before today, Ava had viewed free-floating rental bikes as "urban junk" littering the cityscape. She would never view the bikes the same way again. They were a gift from the heavens… there when you needed them.

She parked the bike next to the metro station and dashed down the stairs. There were only four stops from Odeon to Jussieu. By the time her metro car reached Jussieu, a station in the 5th arrondissement near the *Jardin des Plantes* and the Science University, she was calmer.

Henri's accident couldn't have been that serious, or he wouldn't have been able to text her. The fact that he was in a private clinic and not a public hospital also indicated that it wasn't a life or death situation.

As she rode the escalator out of the station, Ava took several deep breaths.

What Henri's accident showed is that you had to live each day fully. Yesterday Henri had been at a wine tasting, and today he was in a clinic.

The clinic was across from the Jardin des Plantes, Paris's oldest botanical garden. The garden also had a small zoo dedicated to endangered species. Ava walked quickly. As she strode past the fountain across from the botanical garden -- a large stone fountain with a naked woman surrounded by a lion, marine animals and strange stone crocodiles -- she heard a voice call her name.

Puzzled, Ava eyed the statue.

The voice called her name again.

Frowning, Ava looked up. It wasn't the voice of a statue that had come to life. It was a voice she recognized: it was Henri's voice.

Confused, she spun around.

To her astonishment, Henri was sitting at an outdoor table at the café next to the fountain sipping a coffee. Ava walked up to him in disbelief.

"What are you doing here?" Ava demanded as Henri rose and gave her the traditional kisses on her cheeks.

Henri sank back into his chair. "The clinic was crowded. I decided to wait for you here. If you listen, you can hear the animals in the zoo."

Ava sat down across from him. When a lion roared, she didn't know whether to be grateful or angry. She opted for laughter mixed with tears.

Henri was startled. "Ava. What is it?"

"When I got your text, I assumed you were the one who

had an accident. I'm so happy I was wrong."

Henri raised his hand and called the waiter. "What do you want?"

"A café crème and a croissant," Ava said. She had thought of ordering two croissants but realized that would be overkill.

The waiter took her order and left.

Ava sat back in her chair. "Who had an accident?"

"Marc Virgile," Henri announced.

"And he contacted you?" Ava asked, bewildered.

"Yes. He texted me late last night," Henri responded. "I'm as surprised as you are."

They both fell silent as the waiter served her. Immediately, Ava bit into her croissant. As it melted in her mouth, she felt better.

Henri took out his phone and showed her Marc Virgile's text message that had been sent at 1 a.m.:

Had accident. Need to see you tomorrow at clinic across from Jardin des Plantes.

Ava raised her eyebrows. "Why you?"

Henri shrugged. "We'll soon find out."

Ava sipped her café crème. Suddenly, she opened her eyes wide. "I forgot to tell you…"

"One of the people from the tasting contacted you," Henri announced as he sipped his coffee.

Ava was flabbergasted. "How did you know that?"

Henri smiled. "Because I had two friends from Bordeaux call me first thing this morning about helping their friends."

"Roger Allard, the wine broker?"

"Roger Allard, the wine broker, and François Croix," Henri said with a nod. "Although my friend told me to steer clear of François."

"Now it's your turn. Guess who contacted me," Ava said.

"Well, it might be Roger Allard, but I don't see him contacting a woman. That only leaves Lee Baresi, Diane de la Floch or François Croix. I'll go with Diane or Lee."

Ava leaned forward. "Diane! She played the card of female solidarity."

"She's not entirely wrong," Henri responded.

Ava raised her eyebrows. "What do you mean?"

"I don't doubt that the men might join together to win," Henri said. "They could always divide the wine among themselves afterwards."

"Win. That's the same word Diane used," Ava said, puzzled.

"Marc Virgile has set up a contest. It isn't about the wine. It's about dominance. Diane comes from a prominent family, but she got pushed out of the winery because she's a woman. She'll never forget that."

"She told me that she holds the votes to push François out."

"If her cousins agree with her," Henri said. "I'm afraid that she'll have a long wait unless François does something crazy."

"You don't have a very high opinion of François."

Henri nodded. "In addition to my friend's warning, there was something about him that rubbed me the wrong way last night."

"Why did Marc Virgile set up the wine sale as a contest?"

Henri thought before speaking. "Because he could. His family has owned the winery for over a century. I'm sure a lot of bad blood exists between his family and the others. In small communities, people don't forget."

"And Lee?" Ava asked.

"He's the joker. He can align himself with one or all of them. Or none… We'll have to watch Lee. He struck me as very smart." Henri stood up. "It's time to see what Marc wants."

Ava took a last bite of her croissant and jumped to her feet. "Why didn't you tell me that Nate was in Paris?"

Henri's eyes twinkled. "And spoil the surprise?"

"It was a nice surprise," Ava admitted. "Really lovely."

Walking past the fountain, Henri pointed at a crocodile whose head was turned backwards. "Anatomically, crocodiles can't turn their head like that."

Ava eyed the stone animal. She had no doubt that Henri was right. He always was.

The moment Henri and Ava entered the clinic, the silent sound of illness surrounded them. People spoke in whispers. Others filled out forms as they sat nervously in metal chairs waiting to be called.

Henri strode up to the reception desk where a combative couple in their seventies were arguing with the receptionist, a stern-looking woman with short black hair who was visibly annoyed.

"I've told you three times. Visiting hours begin at 1 p.m. You'll have to come back then," the receptionist barked.

The man gripped the reception desk, angry. "We've come all the way from the south of France to see my brother. I'm not leaving until I see him."

The receptionist pursed her lips. "Rules are rules. You'll have to wait! No exceptions."

The man's face grew red. Just as he was about to explode, Henri stepped forward and spoke to the couple.

"If I may… There's a charming café across the street where you can wait. You might even take a stroll in the botanical garden. It's beautiful this time of year."

Grateful to Henri for diffusing a volatile situation, the man's wife smiled. "Thank you. We'll do that." When her husband didn't budge, she pulled on his arm. Reluctantly, he followed her to the exit.

The receptionist watched the couple leave before turning her attention to Henri. "It's like that every day. Rules are there for a reason. How can I help you?"

Henri smiled his best notary smile. "We've come to see one of your patients."

The receptionist arched her eyebrows, ready for war.

"Mr. Virgile is expecting us," Henri said.

Hearing the name, the woman's attitude changed instantly. Flustered, she tapped a key on the computer and wrote a number on a piece of paper. "Mr. Virgile… Of course. Mr. Virgile can have visitors whenever he wants." She handed the paper to Henri and pointed to the elevator. "Mr. Virgile is on the top floor. Turn left when you get off the elevator and go to the end of the hallway."

"You've been very helpful," Henri said with a courteous nod of his head.

The woman beamed. "I try."

Ava watched their interaction, amazed. Once again, Henri's charm had worked. If he could bottle it, he'd be a millionaire.

Alone in the elevator, Henri answered Ava's unasked question. "Marc Virgile's cousin owns the clinic."

The sixth floor was the clinic's top floor. Stepping out of the elevator, everything was quiet. Henri and Ava walked down the hallway. At the end, Henri stopped and knocked on a door that was ajar.

"Come in!" Marc Virgile shouted.

Ava and Henri stepped into the room. It was a VIP suite. It had a wonderful view of the trees in the Jardin des Plantes across the street. It was divided into a bedroom and a large sitting room. Marc Virgile was seated in pajamas and a navy blue terry cloth robe on a low-slung couch in the sitting room section. He was on the phone. "I'll call you back later," he told the person on the other end and hung up. "Sit down. Sit down."

Henri slid into an armchair. Ava sat in a straight back chair next to him.

"Are you ill?" Henri asked.

"Ill? I've never felt better in my life. You don't have a cigar on you, do you? I'd give my soul for a Davidoff," Marc sighed. "I suppose it can wait..."

"What happened to you? You were in fine form last night at the tasting," Henri said.

Marc harrumphed. "You mean I was an impossible old coot. I know who I am. I never pretended to be anything else. DR's death hit me hard. It showed me that we're all mortal. And that time waits for no man..."

Ava studied Marc Virgile's face. He looked sincere.

Henri leaned forward. "You said you had an accident. What happened?"

Marc sighed. "After the tasting, I had dinner with a friend at the Place de Clichy. Afterwards, I was standing at a red light when someone pushed me into the street. I fell, but was able to roll out of the way of traffic. I learned that from watching television." Marc rubbed his shoulder and winced. "What they don't tell you on TV is that it hurts like hell. So I called my cousin. They did some X-Rays. I'm fine. I spent the night here. I didn't want to die in my sleep when I have something important coming up."

Henri looked amused and worried at the same time. "Was it deliberate?"

"It was a beautiful night. There were a lot of people out. But someone pushed me. I didn't fall. I assume it was deliberate," Marc said as he sat back. "They're giving me a scan this morning. Once that's done, I'll be leaving."

"Why did you call me?" Henri asked.

Marc looked around. Satisfied that they were alone, he spoke, "Two reasons… One: I want the sale to go well. This is my last sale. After that, I'm handing everything to my nephew. Plus, I called my friends in Bordeaux and asked about you."

Henri's eyes twinkled.

"Most said that said you were Bordeaux's best notary and that you gave it up to sell books. One mentioned offhand that you did some part-time detective work assisted by a fellow bookseller named Sext." Marc Virgile frowned and stared at Ava. "You seem young to have worked for Scotland Yard."

Ava spoke for the first time. "That was my uncle."

A veil of disappointment crossed Marc's face. "So you're just a bookseller?"

Henri shook his head. "Ava is much more than a bookseller. She inherited her uncle's flair for detective work. She and I have worked on several cases together."

Marc cleared his throat. "That's what I needed to hear. I want the sale to go well. You're to help me choose the best buyer. David, DR," the older man said with great sadness, "used to do that for me. Whenever DR sold my wines, he'd try and discover the reasons the potential buyers want to purchase them. I want these wines to go to someone who will appreciate them, who will keep them… someone who is worthy of them. I don't want some millionaire who will drink them on a yacht with a cheeseburger or flip them in a month… Or worse."

Ava wondered what Henri meant by "worse", but as he didn't venture down that path, she let it go.

Henri shook his head, puzzled. "You must know the people who were at the tasting. The wine world is small. Burgundy is even smaller."

"I only know the persona that they present to the world. Both you and I know how easy it is to live a lie. Some people live a lie their whole life…" Marc's voice trailed off as if the whole process exhausted him. "I'd also like to know which of them is trying to kill me."

The older man's words startled Henri. "Why do you think it's one of them?"

"Instinct… I may be wrong," Marc said.

"Do you think DR was murdered?" Ava asked.

Marc was bewildered. "What? Absolutely not. Why would someone kill DR? His death was an accident."

"That's not what you said at the tasting," Ava protested.

"I said that to wind them up," Marc responded with a mischievous smile.

Henri knitted his brows and eyed the older man. "Why would someone want to kill you?"

"Ask me no questions, and I'll tell you no lies…" Marc said in a tone that implied he had a very good idea of why someone might want to kill him.

Henri leaned forward, a serious look on his face. "What is the second thing you want us to do?"

"Keep them from killing each other," Marc replied, before breaking out into hearty laughter that made his whole body shake.

Ava failed to find the humor in the older man's words.

Suddenly, the door burst open. A thin, wiry man in his early-thirties with dark curly hair, dressed in city shorts and a polo shirt stormed into the room. He positioned himself in front of Marc. He was so angry, he was shaking.

"When were you going to tell me about the sale?" the young man asked, incensed.

Marc shook his head in false dismay. "Yes. I'm fine. Thank you for your concern."

The young man continued to rage, "I don't believe for a moment that you were pushed into traffic. You're just here to egg me on. I'll die before you do…"

Marc waved his hand at the younger man. "Let me introduce you to my nephew, Aymeric Virgile."

Glowering, Aymeric swung toward Henri and Ava. "I suppose you're the potential buyers?"

Ava squared off with Aymeric. "Not at all, we're booksellers. I'm Ava Sext, and this is Henri DeAth."

Aymeric was so startled that he stopped yelling. He blinked several times in disbelief. "Booksellers?"

"Our stands are on the Quai Malaquais," Henri added with a warm smile.

Suspicious, Aymeric turned to his uncle. "I've never seen you read a book in your life."

"And I have no intention of starting now," Marc responded leaving his nephew even more confused. "Henri and Ava are going to help me with the sale."

Aymeric stared at Henri and Ava. "What do they know

about wine?"

Marc chuckled. "Nothing. I'm hoping they'll bring some common sense to the whole affair. Something that you are clearly lacking." He rose to his feet and faced down his nephew. "Domaine de Kirjac will be yours. But not yet… I'm having one more sale. And let me remind you that even after I turn the winery over to you, its private cellar will still belong to me. I promise I won't sell any more bottles. In exchange, I want you to stop interfering. And I want you stop all the rest, or I might change my mind about turning the winery over to you."

Aymeric turned pale. "You're threatening me?"

Marc sighed. "Take it anyway you want. I expect you to stop."

Aymeric bit his lip. "I'm not leaving you in Paris alone."

"Do whatever you want just stay out of my business," the older man said. Suddenly, he exploded with rage. "I don't want any more incidents like last year's…"

Aymeric didn't know what to say. "But uncle… I'm only trying to help."

Marc shook his head. "Which you aren't doing. Go back to Burgundy. Remain in Paris. I don't care. But stay out of my way."

Aymeric opened his mouth to respond. Instead, he fell silent, looked at everyone and walked off without a word.

Exhausted, Marc sank into his chair. "He's even more

pig-headed than I am. The young have to kill the old to survive. But sometimes it's too soon."

A nurse appeared at the door. "It's time for your scan, Mr. Virgile."

Marc turned to Henri and Ava. "Find out who the best buyer is… and if something does happen to me, don't let my murder go unpunished."

Marc stood up and walked off with the nurse.

Worried, Ava turned to Henri. "What are we going to do?"

"I suggest you go back to the bookstand and see who else turns up. I'm having lunch with Roger Allard."

Thinking of the wine broker, Ava frowned. "Maybe you should take a taster with you."

Henri laughed. "I promise you. I'll make it through lunch."

"It's the dessert I'm worried about…"

CHAPTER 12

Why would someone try and kill Marc Virgile? As Ava waved good-bye to Henri as he climbed into a taxi on his way to meet Roger Allard, she couldn't get the question out of her mind.

Marc clearly knew the answer but had no intention of telling them.

Ava examined the question from every angle as she made her way through the meandering streets in the Latin Quarter on her way to her stand. The most obvious answer was Marc's personality. He was abrasive, rude and over-bearing. However, if people were killed for those qualities, a good 25% of Parisians would be dead, if not more.

No… The answer lay elsewhere.

As she crossed the Place Maubert, home in the Middle Ages to ill-famed taverns and bandits ready to slit your throat and now the site of a wonderful outdoor food market, Ava focused on Henri's favorite motives: love and money.

Perhaps Marc Virgile had cheated people in his business dealings… If that were the case, the other party might be angry enough to kill him. But it would be hard to keep a bad deal quiet in Burgundy. If there was a deal gone wrong, Henri would get wind of it.

Then there was love… That was harder to imagine. Marc was in his 70s. Many people found love in later life. However, Marc's cranky personality seemed to preclude romance. But as Ava's late uncle used to say: *never say never.*

So love might be at the heart of the situation…

Then there was Aymeric, the nephew. His uncle's treatment of him today was dismissive and humiliating. Aymeric's treatment of his uncle was condescending and bullying. In her opinion, the two deserved each other.

Finally, there was a last possibility. Marc Virgile's accident was simply an accident.

For a sleuth, that was a depressing outcome.

When she reached the Boulevard St. Michel, Ava crossed through traffic and strode past the pink marble fountain topped with the bronze figures of the Archangel Michael wrestling with the devil. She paused and studied the heroic struggle between the two enemies. In her opinion, the archangel appeared a tad too confident of his victory over his adversary. After all, the devil had proved to be very resilient over the ages.

Ava sighed.

If only life were as easy as a duel between good and evil. In real life, nothing was black and white. Everything was cast in varying shades of grey.

Continuing toward her stand, Ava entered the narrow winding rue Saint-André-des-Arts, a street dating from the 13th century. It was her favorite street in Paris. Despite the problem at hand, she popped into the herbal shop with its old fashioned wooden shelves lined with mysterious white bags of dried herbs. Immediately, the odor of rosemary, anise, lavender and thyme enveloped her. She took a deep breath and then another. The scent was heavenly.

Rejuvenated, she stepped back outside and headed to a tiny hole-in-the-wall jewelry shop. She stared at the handmade Mexican silver bangle bracelets in the window as she had often done. She imagined them dangling around her wrist. The bracelets would be perfect for the rentrée.

Entering the shop, she tried them on. They were perfect. No, they were more than perfect. They were meant to be hers. When this case was solved, Ava would reward herself with them.

With new resolve, Ava left the shop.

However, solving the case was easier said than done. To solve it, she needed more information. Something Marc Virgile said came back to her: some people live a lie their whole life.

Was he referring to anyone in particular? Was he referring to himself?

Ava weighed her options. One: She could open her stand and wait for someone else to come by to try and bribe her. Two: She could go to DR's apartment and see what she could discover. She opted for the proactive response. She would go to Montmartre.

Plunging her hand in her handbag, she dug around until she found the keys to DR's place. Finding them, she gripped them tightly.

Serendipity!

She didn't even remember putting them in her handbag. Finding them meant she could go directly to DR's.

Ava turned, walked down to the quay, crossed the Pont Neuf Bridge and hurried to the busy rue de Rivoli. She caught the 67 Bus and settled into a seat near an open window. The bus would take her to the bottom of Montmartre. From there, she would walk up to the funicular and take it to the top.

When the lumbering bus entered the steep rue de Martyrs, a foodie paradise with cheese shops, fish mongers and bakeries with window displays filled with colorful mouth-watering pastries, Ava had to stop herself from jumping off to buy some.

At the top of the rue des Martyrs, she got off the bus, crossed the busy boulevard and entered the streets of lower Montmartre. As she wound her way through the crowds of people hunting through the discount clothing shops' outdoor stands, her stomach growled.

When she reached the base of the Butte Montmartre, her stomach growled again.

It was time to eat something.

Swirling around, she sauntered over to a crepe stand and lined up behind the tourists. There was something infectious about their enthusiasm for the city. By the time, her *creme de marron* -- chestnut cream -- crepe came wrapped in white paper, Ava felt like she was on holiday. If she didn't have a potential crime to solve she would have gladly taken her crepe to the park across the street and listened to the organ grinder playing "La Vie en Rose".

Instead, she sauntered slowly down the street toward the Marché St. Pierre. From there, she walked to the French Corkscrew, DR's wine shop, and peered through the window.

To her astonishment, Solange Vitrang was on a ladder at the back of the shop.

Finding the door locked, Ava knocked loudly.

When she heard the knocking, Solange climbed down the ladder, looked at the door, strode over and unlocked it. Seeing the crepe in Ava's hand, she grinned. "You didn't buy me one by chance?"

The two women laughed.

"I'll make us some coffee," Solange said, heading to the back of the shop. "I'm glad to see you. I thought I was the last Parisian in Paris."

Ava shook her head. "I hardly qualify as a Parisian."

"Nonsense. Being a Parisian is a state of mind. You're more Parisian than I'll ever be. My Belgium accent is anathema to Parisians. It's all they can do not to burst out laughing. You, on the other hand, have a posh British accent.

Who is more Parisian than Jane Birkin?" Solange asked, referring to the English singer and actress who was a muse to the late Serge Gainsbourg, an iconic French singer-songwriter. "Jane is the very essence of the French girl!"

"What are you doing here?" Ava asked, taking another bite of her crepe.

"After last night's disaster, I probably should have fled. But I'm made of sterner stuff."

"Disaster?" Ava asked, surprised. "Was it that bad?"

"Marc Virgile treated me as if I were some lowly intern. François Croix pretended I didn't exist, and Roger Allard and Diane de la Floch were dismissive. Other than that, the evening went well. Not to mention Marc's accusations that someone there wanted to kill DR. That's preposterous!" Visibly annoyed, Solange poured water into an expensive espresso machine that was identical to the one at DR's apartment. She was so angry she was shaking.

"I didn't know what to expect when I met Marc Virgile," Ava confessed. "I'm glad you and Lee Baresi warned me about him."

Solange shook her head. "Marc's known for mistreating people. Some day, someone's going to wring his neck."

Ava hid her surprise at the woman's virulence. When the espresso was made, Solange handed Ava a cup and saucer and then took hers. Ava was astonished. The cup and saucer were expensive porcelain from Hermes, a top luxury brand.

Seeing Ava's expression, Solange explained, "DR liked

the finest and had the means to buy it."

The two women took their coffees, went to the front of the shop and sat down around the tasting table.

"I don't envy you cataloguing his books. Garance asked me to take an inventory of the wines here. It's so boring. The way it's going, I'll be here until midnight."

"Didn't he have a computer inventory?" Ava asked.

Solange shook her head. "DR was not tech savvy at all. He has numbers on pieces of paper for each wine."

Yet he supposedly preprogrammed an email before his death, Ava thought. So much for that theory…

Solange sipped her coffee. "You and Henri made quite an impression on Marc. He invited you to the dinner."

Ava shook her head. "Henri is the reason for that. People adore him. And Marc invited you."

"Only to annoy Roger Allard and the others," Solange said with a sigh. "I wish I had the means to buy his wine. Some day…" Suddenly, a tear rolled down her face. "I'm sorry. I still can't get over DR's death. Yesterday was the first time I'd been back to the shop. It wasn't easy."

"Lee Baresi talked about DR's special gift. Can you explain more?" Ava asked.

Solange's face lit up. "DR was a super taster."

Ava looked bewildered.

Solange shook her head. " Sorry. I've been in the wine world for so long, I forget that not everyone is familiar with the jargon. A super taster is someone who has incredibly sensitive taste buds. DR, for example, could drink a wine and identify it years later. It's a rare gift. Very few people have it."

"Like perfume makers who can break a perfume down into its elements after one whiff?" Ava asked.

Solange nodded. "Exactly. And don't be fooled by last night's blind tasting. In a real blind tasting where participants had no idea which wine they were drinking, very few people… even the person who owns the vineyard, would be able to say which wine was which. That's why DR was so respected in the high-end wine world. He had a gift that reassured people. He was a legend."

Ava sighed. "I was out of my depth last night. In my tasting notebook, I wanted to write "great", "fantastic" and "marvelous"."

Solange smiled. "There's nothing wrong with that. It comes from the heart."

"Or the palate," Ava teased.

Solange burst out laughing.

Ava grinned. She hoped when this was over that she and Solange could become friends. Ava didn't have any French women friends. Solange was a perfect candidate. She was warm and intelligent. However, she was also linked to the dead man in a mysterious way that Ava needed to discover.

Solange sipped her coffee. "I was also out of my depth

last night. I've written on Burgundy wine. I've tasted Grand Crus, but I've never been invited to an exclusive tasting of Domaine de Kirjac Grand Crus. That said, there's a lot of smoke and mirrors to wine. What makes a good wine? What makes a great wine? I call it wine voodoo."

"Wasn't there outrage in France where they held a blind tasting of California wines and French wines, and California wines came out ahead?" Ava asked.

Solange nodded. "1976. Steven Spurrier, a British wine merchant, held the competition. There were two tastings. The first was for whites. The second was for reds from Bordeaux and Cabernet Sauvignon wines from California. The tasting is known as "The Judgment of Paris" after the Greek myth."

"Marc Virgile must have been relieved that they didn't taste wine from Burgundy," Ava said.

Solange let out a peel of laughter.

"What do you think of Garance?" Ava asked.

Solange shrugged. "She's mysterious. DR mentioned her once or twice. But he hated "officialdom". That's what he called lawyers and notaries."

"You can't be French without having a notary," Ava countered.

"Touché," Solange replied. "They're the bane of our existence. Except for Henri, of course. He's charming. What did you think of the tasting?"

"The wine or the people there?" Ava asked.

Solange gave a lopsided grin. "You understand me. I like that. I hate dim-witted people. You aren't among them."

"Had you met the people before," Ava asked.

"Of course. I wrote on Burgundy wines. François was very helpful about the history of his winery. I was surprised to see him as he and DR had a falling out."

"About what?" Ava asked, trying to hide her extreme interest in the news.

"You'll have to ask François. I just know that they were at daggers' edge before DR died," Solange replied.

"And Diane de la Floch?"

An angry expression flashed across Solange's face. "She married money and thinks she's better than everyone else. After I wrote on François's winery, she lit into me at an industry event, telling me that I got it all wrong." Solange crossed her arms. "I didn't. Diane was on her best behavior last night. Don't be fooled. She's a viper! When I asked to interview Roger Allard for my book, he pretended he didn't have time to see me and set me up with his assistant. I was furious."

Ava was surprised by the woman's virulent opinions.

Solange eyed Ava and shook her head. "Sorry. I got carried away. I haven't been treated very well by the Burgundy wine world… except DR."

"What about Marc Virgile?" Ava asked.

Solange smiled, her anger gone. "Despite being close to

DR, Marc Virgile didn't even bother getting back to me when I asked to interview him. I didn't take it personally. He's like that with everyone. As for Lee Baresi, I've seen him here and there. He represents wealthy buyers. That's probably why DR invited him."

Ava took her last bite of the crepe and crumpled the white paper up and put it next to her cup. "How did DR meet Marc Virgile?"

"They've known each other for ages. I never asked DR how they met. DR was not a man who tolerated questions. Maybe that's what he has in common with Marc."

Solange's remark surprised Ava. Up till now, Solange had seemed to be DR's best friend. This was another take on their relationship. Sensing Solange wanted to get back to work, Ava asked the question that was bothering her. "Do you think DR sent the email?

Solange hesitated. "Ever since I received it, I've been asking myself the same question. My conclusion is that he did. I suspect that DR had planned the whole thing out with Marc Virgile before he died. And when the invitation came, Marc, though surprised, decided to continue with their plan."

"Is that a good idea?"

Solange stood up. "We'll see on Saturday. Let me know if you find anything interesting at DR's."

"Like the numbers to a secret Swiss bank account?" Ava joked.

Startled, Solange stared at Ava. "Do you often find those

in your work?"

Ava laughed. "So far never. But there's always a first time… What book appraisers are sure to find are books, books and more books."

Solange relaxed. The tension disappeared. "I'd better get back to work if I want to finish this today." She walked Ava to the door and unlocked it. "I'll see you on Saturday. Give me your cell phone number if I need to get in touch."

The women exchanged numbers. Ava left the shop without looking back. She had hit the nail on the head with her remark about the bank account. But what did Solange's reaction mean?

Ava headed to the funicular. Maybe she would find the number of a Swiss bank account, but if she did, it would be a first in the history of book appraisals.

CHAPTER 13

Take book off shelf. Shake book to see if anything is inside. Page through book looking for any secret messages. Check book's condition: Does it have its dust jacket? Is it a first or signed edition? Enter data into form on phone. Rinse and repeat.

For the last two hours, Ava had been examining DR's books. The first part of the process -- the shaking and hunting for secret messages related to her sleuthing activities. The rest fell under the appraisal process.

So far, Ava hadn't found anything hidden inside DR's books nor any messages written in the margins. However, as there were shelves and shelves of books left to catalogue, hope sprang eternal.

Still hungry and wishing she had bought two crepes, Ava went to the kitchen and made herself a coffee using DR's fancy espresso machine. Hunting through the kitchen cupboards, she found a porcelain cup and saucer from Hermes, identical to the one at the wine shop.

DR did have expensive tastes.

Coffee in hand, Ava wandered around the apartment

picking up things and putting them down. Nothing she saw gave her any insight into what was going on.

Ava finished her coffee and went back to the bookshelves. She climbed up the ladder, grabbed an armful of books and carried them into a small alcove between the kitchen and the living room. She piled the books up on a table. She chose a playlist from her phone, put her ear buds in her ears and began to work.

After she finished the books, she returned to the living room and climbed up the ladder again, listening to one of her favorite songs.

Suddenly, she sensed a presence.

Someone else was in the room with her.

Startled, she swung around to see who it was and lost her balance. The phrase "it happened so fast" ran through her mind as she fell. She hit the floor hard, and everything went dark.

"Are you OK?"

Ava blinked. She was sitting on the floor in DR's living room, propped up by two cushions. Aymeric Virgile was crouched in front of her with a concerned look on his face.

"What are you doing here?" Ava asked as she sat up. She winced and raised her hand to her shoulder. It hurt.

"Wait right there," Aymeric said. Seconds later, he was back with ice wrapped in a tea towel.

Ava took it and held it to the sore area. Relief was instantaneous. "You didn't answer my question. What are you doing here? How did you get inside?"

"A "thank you" would be appreciated. You're lucky I found you. Did you fall?"

"Yes. I fell," Ava said. "I certainly wasn't taking a nap. I was on the ladder, someone startled me, and I fell. That person wasn't you by any chance?"

The expression on Aymeric's face changed instantly. He was incensed. "Of course, it wasn't me. I just got here. I found you on the floor, dazed. I guessed you'd slipped off the ladder. When I tried to help you, you swore a blue streak and tried to punch me."

Ava grimaced. She didn't remember any of that. She wondered what else she had forgotten.

"You even accused me of attacking you."

"Sorry. And thank you," Ava said. "But you didn't answer my question. How did you get into the apartment?"

"The door was wide open," Aymeric announced as if it was obvious.

Ava rose to her feet. The blood rushed to her head, and she started to fall. Aymeric caught her.

"Easy does it," he said as he helped her to the couch. He handed the ice pack to Ava who put it under her shoulder and leaned back.

"I'm surprised to see you here," Aymeric said in an

accusatory tone.

"Who did you expect to see?"

Aymeric swirled and stared at her as if she had asked a ridiculous question. "David Rose, of course. This is his apartment."

Ava was speechless for a few seconds. "David Rose?"

"If my uncle won't stop this ridiculous sale, David has to," Aymeric said.

"How could David, DR, help?"

"He and Marc are thick as thieves. My uncle would never sell wine from the cellar if David Rose wasn't involved."

"Sit down. I have some bad news for you."

Bewildered, Aymeric look straight at Ava and crossed his arms. "And that is?"

"David Rose is dead. He died three months ago."

The blood flowed out of Aymeric's face. He sank onto a chair. "I didn't know that. How did he die?"

"He fell down the steps next to the funicular."

"An accident?" Aymeric whispered, waiting for the answer.

"An accident," Ava confirmed. "Why would it be anything else?"

Aymeric reared back. "Maybe because last night

someone pushed my uncle into traffic."

"Your uncle's fall could have been accidental," Ava argued.

Aymeric stared at her. "The person who caused you to fall and didn't stick around wasn't an accident. Unless you staged it as you knew I would come by… which is impossible."

"Did you go by the wine shop?"

Aymeric nodded. "No one was there. To be honest, I didn't expect to find David at home, but I had to try."

"How did you get into the building without the code?"

Aymeric looked away. "I have a key."

"To David's apartment?" Ava asked, astounded.

"To the building. A fireman's key."

Ava nodded. Every building entrance door with a code in Paris had a lock beneath it that would open with a single key that firemen and emergency workers possessed. "Where did you get it?"

"At the Porte de Clingancourt flea market. I studied art history when I was a student in Paris. The only way to get inside old buildings to see architectural details was with a key."

"That's illegal!" Ava protested.

Aymeric shook his head. "We're in France. There is the

truly illegal, the slightly illegal and the tolerated illegal. My key falls into the third category."

"Why didn't your uncle tell you about DR's death?"

Aymeric sighed. "As you saw, we're not really on the same wavelength. He only chose me to take over the winery because I'm a Virgile."

"What did your uncle mean when he told you to not to do anything like you did last year?"

Aymeric narrowed his eyes and looked at her strangely. "For a book seller, you're very inquisitive."

Ava moved the ice pack and sat up straight. "Having an active mind is part of the job."

"That must be why my uncle asked you to the dinner," Aymeric said, still wary.

"He asked Henri. I'm just going along for the ride."

"Who else was invited?"

"You'll have to ask your uncle. I'm not at liberty to say," Ava responded.

"Will I have to walk over hot coals to get information from you?" Aymeric asked.

Ava ignored his remark. "How did you find out about the sale?"

Aymeric shook his head. "Two can play at this game. I'm not going to tell you."

"Are you always this stubborn?"

"I could be worse. I'm my uncle's nephew."

Ava looked at him. Aymeric looked nothing like his uncle. In other circumstances she would have said he was good-looking. Given the situation, she downgraded that to not bad-looking.

"What are you going to do now?"

"Try and find out what's going on and keep my uncle alive. If he dies now, I get nothing."

"So much for family love."

Aymeric burst out laughing. "Family love? You don't know the Virgiles. I respect my uncle. I can't say I love him."

Ava shook her head. It was clear that both uncle and nephew were fond of each other, although they would never admit it.

"But family is family, and a Virgile is a Virgile," Aymeric said with the weight of the world on his shoulders.

"Will we be seeing you on Saturday?" Ava asked.

"Not if my uncle can help it."

Ava stood up. She felt queasy.

Concerned, Aymeric looked at her. "You need to go home and get some sleep. I'll call you a taxi. In fact, I'll call both of us a taxi."

"What are you going to do?"

"Try and make sense out of what's going on. But as it involves my uncle who defies logic, it won't be easy."

CHAPTER 14

The sky was dark, the moon was the barest sliver, and the apartment was silent. Ava eyed the glass roof overhead and wondered how long she had been sleeping. She sat up on the couch, pulled the colorful quilt she had bought at an American craft fair in London tightly around her and eyed the clock.

It was midnight.

She had been sleeping ever since she had returned from DR's place and her brush with an intruder… if there had been an intruder. Ava was confident that Aymeric had found the door open as he had said, but until she was one hundred percent certain, she couldn't rule out the possibility that he had been the one who had startled her.

Rising to her feet, she looked down and eyed her attire. She was happy to see that she had changed into her summer pajamas -- a bright yellow T-shirt with matching shorts. She walked to the table, grabbed her handbag, took her phone out and ran through the messages.

A text from Henri suggested breakfast at 9:30 at a café near the Palais Royal Gardens. She texted him back a brief

"OK".

There were also several calls from Nate asking her to call him. This behavior was so unlike Nate that Ava was troubled. Normally, he would call her once and wait for her to get back to him.

She dialed his number. It was the same time in Rome. Nate would be up as he never went to bed early.

His number rang once, twice, and then a third time.

Ava was about to hang up when Nate answered.

"Ava?" His voice was tense.

"The very same," Ava responded, trying to sound stronger than she felt.

"I was worried about you."

Now Ava was really puzzled. Nate never worried about her. How often had he said: You're invincible… It's the criminal who has to worry…?

Now it was Ava's turn to be worried. *What had happened to disturb him?*

He couldn't possibly know about her being attacked… although attacked might be too strong a word. Being hit on the head was an attack. Falling off a ladder when you were a book appraiser was a work accident.

"Ava? Are you there?"

Ava snapped out of her reverie. "I'm here. What's

wrong?"

"When I left this morning, I grabbed your tasting notebook," Nate confessed.

"And you couldn't read my handwriting?" Ava joked. She tried to remember if Nate had seemed stressed yesterday evening. On the contrary, he had never been better.

"It wasn't your handwriting," Nate announced, in a dramatic tone of voice.

"Whose was it?" Ava asked, sure Nate was teasing her.

"I don't know. I wish I did. It might help you and Henri."

Suddenly, Ava's mind cleared in a flash. Something was wrong with the notebook.

"When I got home from work. I opened it. I wanted to see the wines that you had tasted. There were no names of wines, only numbers and incredibly detailed tasting notes and numbers."

"That's because it was a blind tasting. We tasted eight wines."`

"Ava, I can't imagine you writing "sensual, seductive and intense with an intoxicating nose."

"That's because I don't even know what that means," Ava admitted as she hoped the person who had her notebook didn't read her absurdly amateur notes. "It's not my notebook. Why does that worry you?"

"Because the person also wrote *"who did it?"* across the bottom of a page and underlined it twice."

Stunned, Ava fell silent.

"I looked on all the other pages but didn't find anything else like that," Nate said.

"Can you send it to me?" Ava asked as her mind raced.

"I scanned the entire notebook and emailed it to you earlier."

"I adore you? Did I ever tell you that?" Ava told Nate as she leapt up and grabbed her tablet.

"Once or twice. But I'd be happy to hear you say it more often," Nate teased.

Ava opened her email, went directly to Nate's mail and opened the PDF attachment.

"I put the page with the note on it in the beginning. In reality, it was on page six, wine number six. "

Her heart racing, Ava read the first page and then read the through the other pages of notes. There was nothing else in them that was non-wine related.

"What do you think it is about?" Nate asked.

"I have no idea..." Ava reread the scanned pages. Someone who knew wine had written the tasting notes. But then everyone at the tasting knew about wine except her and Henri. Although she had no doubt that Henri knew way more about Burgundy wine than he let on.

"DR's accident?" Nate suggested.

"Maybe. Or it might be referring to the person who sent the email," Ava responded. "Or something else Henri and I don't know about yet.

Suddenly, Nate fell silent. After a few seconds, he spoke. "Why didn't you get back to me right away? That's not like you."

Ava bit her lip and decided the only way Nate could understand the state she was in was to fill him in on her day. "This morning, Diane de la Floch came to my stand to try and bribe me to help her."

"She came right out and offered you money?"

"Yes. She even played the card of female solidarity."

"What did you say?"

"That I'd think about it… Then Henri texted me from the clinic and said there'd been an accident."

"Is he OK?" Nate asked, alarmed.

"It wasn't Henri who had an accident. It was Marc Virgile."

"The owner of Domaine de Kirjac who is holding the wine sale on Saturday?"

"The very same. He was having dinner in a restaurant in Pigalle. After dinner, he was waiting to cross the street at a red light when someone pushed him into the street. He managed to roll out of the way of traffic. He checked himself into his cousin's clinic."

"Do you believe him?"

"Why would Marc lie? It makes no sense. It's possible that it was an accident, except..." Ava stopped. Tears welled up in her eyes.

"Ava, what is it," Nate asked, alarmed.

"After the clinic, I went to Montmartre. I had coffee with Solange at the wine store where she was taking inventory. Then I went to DR's place to work on cataloguing his books. Someone entered the apartment. I was so startled, I fell off the ladder, hit my head and lost consciousness. The worst is I didn't see who it was."

"Are you OK? Did you see a doctor? What did Henri say?" Nate asked, spitting out his words all at once.

"Nate. I'm fine. I haven't told Henri yet. Luckily, Aymeric found me."

"Aymeric? Who the hell is Aymeric?" Nate asked, his voice bristling with anger.

Ava was astonished at Nate's knight in shining armor side. "Aymeric is Marc Virgile's nephew and heir who will take over the winery after the sale. I met him at the clinic."

"What was he doing at DR's?"

"He wanted to talk to him. He didn't know DR was dead..." Ava sighed. "There's a good and a bad side to someone breaking into DR's."

"Start with the bad," Nate said.

Ava smiled. She could imagine Nate pacing back and forth, arms crossed, waiting for her explanation. "The bad is I lost consciousness and didn't see who the intruder was.

"Wasn't it Aymeran?" Nate demanded, deliberately mispronouncing the name.

"Aymeric. And no, it wasn't. The good is I wasn't hurt and the break in means someone is searching for something, and they haven't found it yet."

"Do you know what that is?" Nate asked.

"Off the top of my head, I'd say DR's missing money. Garance is in Singapore looking for it now."

"There's another possibility," Nate said.

"What?"

"Solange told someone that you were going to DR's, and the attack was to scare you."

Ava frowned. "I can't believe Solange would do that. It had to be someone who didn't know I was there. I had my ear buds on and was listening to music so maybe someone did knock on the door, and I didn't hear them. The person must have been as astonished as I was."

"A person who didn't stop to see if you were OK…"

"That's true…"

"Who do you think the notebook belongs to?"

"If I have the person's notebook, that means they have mine. Solange didn't seem odd when I spoke to her. Marc Virgile didn't take notes. Diane wasn't worried this morning. However, it might be that neither Solange nor Diane have noticed that they have the wrong notebook. It could also be Lee Baresi, the wine buyer from New York or François Croix…"

"Diane's cousin who she jilted?" Nate asked.

"Diane didn't jilt him. She just didn't marry him. It's not the same thing," Ava clarified.

"And the last one? The wine broker… What's his name?"

"Roger Allard… Roger contacted a friend in Bordeaux to get an in with Henri. The two had lunch today."

"What did Henri learn?"

"I haven't spoken to him since we saw Marc Virgile at the clinic. We're having breakfast at Palais Royal tomorrow." Ava checked the time. "Sorry, today!"

"What are you going to do now?"

"Open the refrigerator, see if there is any goat's cheese left from last night's fabulous dinner and eat it."

"Is your front door locked?" Nate asked. "I don't want anything to happen to you."

"Nothing will. Except maybe I'll find another dead body or two before the week is out!" Ava announced as she walked to the refrigerator.

Nate laughed. "I'm glad to hear you're back to normal. Text me if you need me. You know where I am."

Ava hung up. She opened the refrigerator and took out the goat's cheese. She smiled when she saw that a handful of cherries was left. Sometimes, good things happen just when you need them.

CHAPTER 15

The smell of freshly baked bread and cinnamon wafted over Ava as she pushed open the door to the café. It was a trendy organic bakery/café on the rue des Archives behind the Palais Royal Gardens. Low jazz was playing in the background. The only other sound was the low tapping sound of fingers on keyboards as people worked on their computers.

Ava, dressed in a striped beige and blue linen dress with her hair pulled up in a ponytail, looked around the café for Henri. He was seated at a window table that had a view of the garden. Today he was wearing jeans and a pink linen shirt and looked chic and simple at the same time.

Happy to see him, Ava walked up to his table. "Are you always on time?"

"Always," Henri said with a grin. He rose to his feet and kissed her on each cheek.

"How did you get this table? It's prime real-estate," Ava asked as she sank into her chair and gazed out at the formal gardens. Despite everything that had happened yesterday, or maybe because of it, Ava had slept like a log. The only reason she hadn't been late for her meeting with Henri was that she had set the alarm and had taken a taxi. While the driver had grumbled throughout the short drive, upset that she wasn't going to the far end of Paris, his mood improved when Ava tipped him generously. Now gazing out over the gardens, Ava felt great… like nothing traumatic had happened the day before.

"How did I get this table? Luck. Sheer luck. I walked through the door, and the person sitting here stood up."

Ava raised her eyebrows. "And?"

"And then I elbowed everyone out of my way to grab it," Henri joked.

"Did you order?"

Henri nodded. "An iced café latte and a butternut squash frittata."

Intrigued by Henri's order, Ava opened the menu and read through it carefully. The choices were overwhelming.

When the waiter appeared Ava closed the menu. "I'll have an iced café latte and a *tartine* -- an open faced sandwich -- with smoked salmon, organic hard-boiled eggs and dill."

"Only that?" Henri teased.

"This was a great choice," Ava said looking around the café.

Henri raised his eyebrows in mock outrage. "Are you insinuating that some of my choices aren’t great?"

"Do you want the truth?" Ava asked.

"No," Henri said.

"What did Roger Allard want?" Ava asked, referring to Henri's lunch the day before with the wine broker.

"Like Diane de la Floch... he wants me to help him win Marc Virgile's favor, if possible. He and Marc have had run ins over the years and worries that will count against him."

Curious, Ava leaned forward. "Run ins?"

The waiter arrived and served them. When he'd left, Henri took a sip of his iced café latte and continued.

"I called around," Henri admitted.

Ava smiled. "I knew you would." If there was one thing she could count on was Henri's network of friends helping them.

"Marc Virgile also makes wine under another name -- *Domaine de la Fin*. It's grown on a parcel of land that belonged to his father once. The father lost it after the war. Marc was able to get the land back ten years ago and is growing wine on it."

"*The End Domaine*? End of what? That's an odd name for a wine," Ava said as she bit into her tartine. The salmon and dill were perfect together. She vowed to buy both ingredients the next time she went shopping.

"Roger Allard was not a big fan of the wine. He trashed it. Marc never forgave him."

"And now?" Ava asked.

"It's become a successful wine," Henri said. "Almost as difficult to find as Domaine de Kirjac, although much less expensive."

"What did you tell Roger?" Ava asked.

"That I'd think about his offer…"

"What?" Ava replied, astounded.

"Isn't that what you told Diane?" Henri asked.

"But I didn't mean it," Ava said.

"Neither did I," Henri replied. "I don't believe that Roger really wanted me to help him."

Ava knitted her brows together. "Then what did he want?"

"To find out why we were there… He asked about you also," Henri said as he bit into his frittata.

Watching an expression of delight run across his face, Ava vowed to order the frittata the next time she came to the café.

"I told him that we often did book appraisals together. He asked me about Garance."

"How did he know about her?"

"That was my question. I didn't ask him, of course. I explained that we had known each other since school. One last thing I learned…"

Ava sipped her iced café latte and waited.

"He and Marc had dinner last night."

Ava's eyes opened wide. "I thought they didn't like each other?"

"They don't," Henri said. "That doesn't mean that they don't have to deal with each other. Burgundy is small."

"Did Roger see the accident?"

Henri shook his head. "If he did, he didn't mention it."

"As he was dining with Marc, he knew where Marc would be…" Ava said, leaning forward. "Roger could have orchestrated the whole thing!"

"Why?"

"Because one of them did it…" Ava responded with a knowing nod.

"What?" Henri asked, bewildered.

"Nate took my tasting notebook to Rome with him by accident yesterday. When he opened it to read about the wines, "who did it?" was written in the margin of one of the pages. He knew it wasn't my notebook because the person wrote that the wine had an intoxicating nose, and I don't even know what that means."

"*Who did it?* was written in the notebook?" Henri asked.

"And underlined twice," Ava said as she took out her phone and showed the pdf to Henri.

He scrolled through the document and put her phone

down. "We have a lot to learn before Saturday. If things continue like this… someone else will have an accident."

Ava swallowed. It was now or never. "Henri, yesterday after I left the clinic, I went up to Montmartre."

Henri was silent. The tone of Ava's voice told him that what she was saying was serious.

"First, I went by the French Corkscrew. Solange was there doing an inventory. We had coffee and spoke."

"Did you learn anything important?"

"She doesn't think DR was killed. Like Diane, she believes it was just Marc trying to wind them up. And she was angry over how everyone treated her."

"She was treated badly. I agree."

"When I joked that I hoped to find the number to a secret bank account, she didn't laugh."

"And then?" Henri asked, sensing that Ava hadn't gotten to the essence of what had happened.

"Then I went to DR's apartment. I spent a very boring two hours going through his books, cataloguing them. I had a coffee. I was on the ladder, heard a noise, turned to see who it was and fell. When I regained consciousness, I was on the floor with Aymeric staring down at me."

A look of astonishment spread over Henri's face. "Why didn't you start with that?"

"Because I don't know what to make of it. Aymeric said

I swore up a storm, accused him of breaking into the apartment and tried to hit him."

"What in heaven's name was Aymeric doing there?"

"He wanted to speak with DR."

Henri was so startled he blinked twice. "Start at the beginning."

Ava told him the whole story. As she spoke, she could see Henri placing the new events into the narrative he was building of the case.

"What's your gut feeling?" Henri asked.

"I wish I could tell you. I'll go with someone entered other than Aymeric. Someone who had a key."

"Did you hear from Garance?" Ava asked.

Henri nodded. "She sent me a text that she had arrived in Singapore, but since then nothing."

"No news is good news?" Ava suggested.

"If there's something to find, Garance will find it. She's a bulldog."

"A very charming one," Ava added. "What did Roger Allard say about the others who were at the tasting?" Ava imagined that the wine broker had a strong opinion about them.

"Burgundy is small. He's known most of them their whole lives. He respects Diane de la Floch. She'll do anything to push François Croix out."

"And François?"

"François believes he's smarter than he is and will eventually trip over his own feet. In Roger's opinion, François isn't particularly interested in running his vineyard, but he likes playing the rich winemaker."

Ava raised her eyebrows. "Is he rich? I know Diane is rich. She told me that she married well and divorced even better."

"It must run in the family. François also married a wealthy woman. A Belgian socialite. They lead separate lives…" Henri's voice trailed off. "To understand winemakers in France, you need to understand the basic economics of wine. There's a joke that explains it all."

Ava leaned forward. "Shoot."

Henri grinned. "What's the best way to make a million euros as a winemaker?"

Ava shrugged. "Tell me."

"Start with five million euros. Wine making is a risky business. You can have a bad year and lose everything. How many people can put millions and millions into a winery and not expect to make the money back for years. Today, wine production is a rich person's game as is wine collecting. Prices of Burgundy Grand Crus have soared, especially old vintages. In many cases, the wines aren't for drinking but are bought as an investment."

"Domaine de Kirjac sells itself," Ava protested.

"Now it does. But it wasn't always like that. Marc Virgile's father had to sell off parcels in the post war years just to keep his main winery. Marc has done a good job. But even for him, it hasn't been easy. He needs to invest massively. Plus, the number of bottles they make each year is small. That's why he bought back parcels and is producing different wines."

Ava thought of Marc Virgile. Even in the clinic, the older man had a larger than life personality.

"More than anything, Marc wants the winery to live on after him. And that's where Aymeric fits into the picture."

Hearing Aymeric's name, Ava sat up straighter, anxious to learn more about her savior.

"Aymeric studied art. He managed the art collection for a famous billionaire. When he decided to accept his uncle's offer, the billionaire offered him a large sum to continue managing the collection, a sum that few people would refuse."

"And?" Ava asked.

"Aymeric refused. Money wasn't as important as a winery that had been in the family for over one hundred years," Henri explained.

"Blood is thicker than money?" Ava suggested tongue-in-cheek.

"Absolutely. Although it's better when they go together."

Ava sat back in her seat. What Henri was telling her changed her opinion of Aymeric. Yes, he could be disagreeable. But he was also giving up a lot for the family winery. Marc Virgile was volatile and could change his mind at any time.

"We need to find out more. Fortunately, we're meeting someone who should be able to throw light on things." Henri raised his hand and signaled for the check.

"We're meeting him now?" Ava asked.

"We're meeting him now," Henri confirmed.

CHAPTER 16

The shop was in the 2nd arrondissement down the street from the Louvre and across from the Banque de France, the French Federal Bank. The neighborhood was quieter than usual as it was August. A few tourists were seated on a café's outdoor terrace soaking in the sun as neighborhood children rode their skateboards up and down in front of them, spinning in circles while doing complicated acrobatic maneuvers.

Henri strolled up the street taking obvious delight in his surroundings. Ava marveled at how Henri was always in touch with what was going on around him. She, on the other hand, was often lost in her thoughts.

"Is your friend's shop nearby?"

Henri nodded. "It's been in the same building for over eighty years. Jean inherited the business from his father who inherited it from his father who inherited it from his father. For all I know, there have been Colberts selling wine from the beginning of time."

"Just like the DeAths have been notaries since the

beginning of time?"

Henri chuckled. "Even earlier… "

He stopped in front of a shop whose windows were frosted over, making it impossible to see inside. *Colbert & Colbert* was written in small letters on the center of the window. Henri walked up to the door and rang the bell.

Seconds later, a chic man Henri's age with thick brown hair, wearing tortoise shell rimmed glasses, jeans and an immaculate white shirt opened the door as he spoke on the phone. "The price is the price. They can take it or leave it. I have to go." The man hung up and hugged Henri warmly. "Henri! It's always a pleasure…"

Henri turned to Ava. "Jean very kindly took time out of his busy schedule to see us."

Jean Colbert guffawed. "Busy? In August? I was looking for any excuse to stop working. If the rentree wasn't coming, I'd be on a tennis court somewhere." He turned to Ava. "I've heard a lot about you. I'm sorry about your uncle. I only met him once but he was a prince among men."

"Uncle Charles was special," Ava said, not surprised at Jean's warm words about her uncle. Charles Sext was uniformly liked.

Jean waved them inside. The room was empty except for a large table with a huge vase of fresh flowers on it. A few bottles of wine were on the table. Otherwise, there was nothing that indicated that Jean Colbert was a wine merchant.

"Before we go up to my office, let me show Ava my

treasures." Jean walked to a door, opened it, and entered several numbers into a screen on the wall. "The alarm system... The insurance company insisted on it."

Henri and Ava followed Jean down the steps to the cellar. Its walls were made of old stone that had been sandblasted white. Wine lined the walls from floor to ceiling. It was a welcoming space. The soft lighting and beautifully stocked shelves made Ava went to explore the room. It was a far cry from the damp, unwelcoming cellar beneath DR's shop.

Jean waved his hand at the wine. "This is only a tiny part of our stock. However, during my grandfather's time, this cellar was Colbert & Colbert." Jean strode over a shelf, took out a bottle and showed its label to Henri. "When was the last time you saw one of these?"

"A 2002 Lafitte Rothschild. You're a man after my own heart..." Henri replied with a grin.

Jean nodded, content. "There are some benefits to working in wine... although with the price of this bottle today, I'd hesitate to drink it. I'd be drinking the family fortune."

"Which wall gives onto the Banque de France? I forget," Henri asked.

Jean pointed to the far wall and grinned at Ava. "The Banque de France is just across the street. France's gold is stocked there in underground vaults. When we were ten, Henri and I spent an entire summer imagining what we'd do if the wall collapsed, and we could steal it."

"You wanted to buy a racecar," Henri said.

"A red one," Jean added with a laugh. "And you wanted a helicopter." He turned to Ava. "I spent my childhood summers in Arcachon. That's how I met Henri. We took sailing lessons together."

Arcachon was a seaside resort on the Atlantic Coast where Bordeaux's bourgeoisie traditionally spent the summer holidays. Its huge Victorian mansions and sand dunes were part of its charm. Ava had been there once and would gladly go back.

"If only life could be that simple," Henri said with a nostalgic sigh.

"How about a glass of wine to celebrate?"

"It depends on which wine," Henri replied with a twinkle in his eye.

"I take that as a challenge," Jean replied as he walked to the far end of the cellar eyeing the shelves. He pulled out a bottle. "A 2012 Chateau Quinault L'Enclos?"

"Drinkable," Henri said with a nod of approval.

Jean burst out laughing. "You haven't changed. As impossible as ever." He eyed Ava. "Henri has always liked the finer things in life."

The trio wound their way up to the ground floor and then continued up the stairs to the next floor. Jean led them into a room that had a massive old-fashioned wooden desk in a corner. A large captain's chair was behind it. Two well-worn leather armchairs stood in front of it. The room was cool. A tall tree in the courtyard shaded it from the hot summer sun.

Henri ran his hand lovingly over the desktop. "You still have your grandfather's desk?"

Jean nodded. "That's the problem with a family business. The past is omnipresent. I would prefer a modern desk, all glass and metal. Every time I even think about it, I can feel my grandfather's eyes bearing down on me," Jean said, pointing to a portrait of a stern-looking man with a white goatee hanging on the wall. "But then, I'm no different. We've outgrown our space here, but I know the neighborhood like the back of my hand. I'd be heartbroken to leave it. We have a state-of-the-art warehouse/office outside Paris. I spend three days a week there and the rest of the time here. So in my own way, I also cling to the past."

Henri settled into one of the armchairs. Ava sat next to him. Jean walked behind the desk and took out three glasses and a corkscrew. He opened the wine, sniffed the cork and handed the bottle to Henri who sniffed it and smiled. As Henri poured the wine, Jean left the room.

"How much does he know?" Ava asked in a low voice.

"I explained the situation. Don't worry. Jean is the soul of discretion," Henri responded.

Jean returned with a tray of cheese, cold cuts and olives. "A pre-lunch appetizer." He pointed at the tray. "Bleu de Basque and Beaufort d'Alpage cheese, Lomo de Bellota sausage and Mangalica ham. And Manzanilla olives…"

Jean lifted his glass for a toast. "To old friends…" He looked at Ava. "…And new acquaintances."

Ava lifted her glass to ger nose. It was heaven.

"What do you smell?" Jean asked her.

Ava looked alarmed. She hoped he wasn't expecting her to analyze the wine. "I'm a novice at this…"

"Don't worry about making a mistake. Too many wine snobs get lost in the terminology. I started tasting when I was six. I never stopped," Jean said.

"Six?" Ava tried to imagine the young Jean tasting wine as a child.

"It was work, not pleasure. When your family is in wine, you need to know it. Luckily, I grew up and am able to enjoy wines away from the pressure."

"How is your father?" Henri asked as he sat back in the leather armchair and took a piece of blue cheese.

"Trekking in the Himalayas." Jean replied. "He's eight-three. I hope I have his stamina at that age."

As everyone sipped their wine, Henri leaned forward. "DR… David Rose… What do you know about him?"

"As I'm specialized in wines from Bordeaux, I didn't have a lot of personal dealings with him. But whenever there were auctions for high-end French wines, he was omnipresent".

"In what capacity?" Henri asked popping an olive into

his mouth.

"Sometimes, he represented anonymous sellers. Other times, he represented anonymous buyers. Sometimes, both… In London and New York, he represented a group of wealthy older men who believe in the finer things in life: gourmet meals, exclusive restaurants, pricey watches, bespoke clothing, and expensive wine… the more expensive the better."

"But DR wasn't a millionaire…" Henri said with raised eyebrows.

"No, but he brought the group an encyclopedic knowledge of high-end wine, an incredible palate and access to rare Grand Cru wines. Money is not enough to buy rare wines. You need to know the right people. DR knew all the right people. And, from all I heard, he thought nothing about bringing thousands of euros of wine to a dinner"

"Where was the money paid?" Henri asked.

Jean took a piece of ham and nibbled on it. "If the wine was sold through Christies or Sotheby's, the payment was to a declared entity. That didn't mean that this entity wasn't a trust in some tax haven. If you're asking me if DR made a lot of money, it depends on what a lot is... What's a pittance for his billionaire friends might be a lot for DR."

Henri frowned. "He bought an apartment in Montmartre for cash that's in the name of an offshore trust."

"How much?" Jean asked.

"A few million euros… " Henri responded.

"In my estimation, he made a lot more than that… But despite the circles he ran in, DR always struck me as down to earth. He wasn't caught up in the hype that surrounded wine."

"What about Marc Virgile?" Henri asked.

Jean slapped his thigh in mirth. "Two more different people couldn't exist. Yet DR and Marc were often seen dining together. Why? They say opposites attract... I never understood their friendship, although I don't doubt it was sincere."

"Did Marc Virgile go to auctions in New York or London?" Ava asked.

Jean shook his head. "Never. He didn't have to. His wine went for him."

"Then where did DR and Marc see each other?" Ava asked.

"Here in Paris. Or in Burgundy," Jean replied. "Marc Virgile isn't known for having friends. He never married. He never had children. Domaine de Kirjac is his life. He's done a fine job. After the war, Marc's father sold parcels of land to pay for his womanizing. Word has it that Marc threatened to kill him if he sold another parcel."

"What happened then?" Henri asked.

"He got lucky. His father fell off a tractor during the harvest and died," Jean said. "If Marc Virgile is difficult, his father was ten times more difficult."

"It wasn't a suspicious death?" Ava asked. In her view, there were a lot of people dying who had come in contact with Marc Virgile.

Jean reared back his head, astonished by her question. "Absolutely not. If you're wondering if Marc had something to do with his father's death, the answer is no. Marc spouts a lot of nonsense, but he wouldn't hurt a fly. From what I know of his father, there were quite a few people who wanted him dead. Marc's father's weakness was other men's wives. Plus, the old man drank a lot."

"How did Marc choose Aymeric to inherit the winery?" Henri asked.

Ava took a piece of ham and listened, curious about her savior -- if he was her savior.

Jean shrugged. "There's no one else. Aymeric is the last of the Virgiles. Marc's sister has children, but they're not Virgiles. Aymeric is highly intelligent. He'll figure it out. The question is why would he want to deal with Marc? The only answer I can find is that he's a Virgile."

"Tell me about Aymeric," Henri said.

"Aymeric's father was a playboy. He died in a car crash when Aymeric was a child. His mother remarried an English aristocrat and moved to London. Aymeric grew up in English boarding schools and went to the university, both in the UK and here in Paris," Jean explained.

"We witnessed a blowup between the two this morning. Marc warned his nephew not to do what he did last year .

What was that about?" Ava asked as Jean poured more wine in their glasses.

"There was a wine sale at an auction house early last year. I don't remember which one. Word has it that Aymeric, who was working at the winery that summer, insisted the bottles were fake as the labels were different from other bottles of the same vintage. Marc was furious."

"What happened?" Ava asked.

"The wine was sold at a great price for a terrible year," Jean replied with a grin. "Sometimes the Gods do smile on you."

"Were they fake?" Henri asked.

"Labels weren't always uniform as they are today. But let's suppose for argument's sake that the wine was fake… You just don't want to open that can of worms," Jean insisted.

Puzzled, Ava frowned. "Why?"

"Because then people would wonder if the rest of your bottles were fake. Prices would plunge. Luckily, Marc was able to hush things up."

Henri sipped his wine. "Do you think the bottles were fake?"

"Fake! Don't even breathe a word like that around Marc. I truly believe if Marc were to taste one of his own wines and discover that it was fake, he would proclaim to the high heavens that it was exceptional… as would any other vintner.

A friend in the wine world once joked: if my fake wine can sell for that much, I wonder what I can get for the real wine? Wine is alive. It changes. No two bottles are the same. For many old wines, the person buying it has never tasted it. For many old wines, even the person who runs the winery might not have tasted it."

"Then how do fakes get caught out?" Ava asked, more and more bewildered.

"The wrong labels. The wrong year. For example, the winery didn't exist, but somehow it made wine… It takes skill and knowledge to pull off a sophisticated fraud. Maybe that's why it's so rare that we hear about it. Besides, if you were a billionaire who bought fake wine, would you want to admit it?"

"Marc is selling off bottles from his cave," Henri announced.

Immediately, Jean's eyes lit up.

"A private sale. He's already preselected the buyers," Henri explained.

Jean eyebrows snapped together. "Let me guess… Diane de la Floch is one of them."

"How did you know?" Ava asked.

"She has money and is building an incredible wine cellar," Jean said with a nod. "Plus, Marc has always had a soft spot for her."

"Does that mean she has an "in" for the wine?" Ava

asked.

Jean burst out laughing. On the contrary, she'll have to fight twice as hard to show she's better than the men. But Marc will respect her for doing that."

Ava was silent. That explained Diane lining up allies to help her get the wine. She would have to fight harder than the men, which didn't seem fair.

"François Croix," Henri said.

Jean's face showed his astonishment. "François? That surprises me from Marc. He doesn't like François. François is a "*fils de papa*".... a daddy's boy. Marc inherited his winery, but he has worked incredibly hard to keep it going. François is running the family winery and is resting on the winery's reputation. That's dangerous."

Ava frowned. "Does he have the money to buy the wine?"

"François's wife is wealthy. Maybe she's loosening the purse strings, although I hear she keeps him on a tight leash. The only reason they don't divorce is that it's easier and cheaper for her to stay together. They lead separate lives, and he is not immune to charming women…" Jean said.

Ava had a hard time imagining François as a ladies' man, but then she had only seen him briefly.

"Who else?" Jean asked.

"Roger Allard," Henri added.

"Perfectly logical. Wealthy. Competitive. He's the most

important broker in Burgundy. He'll do anything to get the wine. Has he already contacted your friends in Bordeaux?"

Henri nodded. "Yes. Roger and I had a wonderful lunch together yesterday."

"The Interalliée or the Automobile Club?" Jean asked, referring to two exclusive members-only clubs in Paris.

"The Automobile Club. We drank champagne to avoid having to choose between Burgundy and Bordeaux," Henri exclaimed.

"*Sacré* Roger! Always diplomatic. I admire him. I wish I could be as cold-blooded as he is, but I prefer to have less money and enjoy life more… although it isn't fashionable to say that," Jean proclaimed.

"Then there's Lee Baresi." Henri added.

Jean shrugged. "I know of him. He's Asian American. He represents a lot of big players. I've never dealt with him. He speaks perfect French, English, German, Italian and Mandarin. He ran in DR's world although they're from different generations."

Henri looked thoughtful.

Ava spoke up, "DR is supposedly the one who chose the potential buyers for the sale, not Marc Virgile. What was DR's relationship to them?"

"As I said, I didn't see DR often. I'm not surprised that he invited Lee, Roger and Diane. Lee ran in his circle. Roger is a major player and Diane has tons of money. François is the odd duck out. But DR might have had a reason for that."

Henri pursed his lips. "Would anyone want to hurt DR?"

Jean's face showed his astonishment. "Physically hurt him? No! Professionally hurt him? It's a tough business."

Henri finished his wine and stood up. "Thank you for taking time to see us."

Jean shook his head. "I enjoyed it… And Henri, if the wall in the cellar does collapse, you'll be the first one I'll call."

Standing in the street, Ava turned to Henri. "What do you think?"

"That we need more information, and we need to find it fast," Henri said, worried.

"Did someone try and hurt Marc Virgile?" Ava asked, still unsure about Marc's accident.

"It's hard to say. Marc is a difficult man to read."

"Even for a notary?"

Henri grinned. "Even for a notary…"

Ava frowned. "What are we going to do now?"

"I'm off to Geneva. I'll be back tomorrow afternoon… I'm seeing a friend who is a notary in Beaune."

"The wine capital of Burgundy?" Ava asked.

Henri nodded.

Ava was puzzled. "Why are you going to Geneva and not Beaune?"

"Because less people will see him in Geneva and those who do will pretend not to. Despite Switzerland's cleaning house against tax fraud, there's still a lot of French money in Swiss banks. Some legitimately. Some not. I'll also be seeing a Swiss friend who might know something. What do intend to do?"

"I'm going to go back to DR's. If someone broke in, it's because there is something that someone is looking for. If it's at DR's, I intend to find it."

"You're not scared about going back?" Henri asked.

Ava grinned. "If I stay off ladders, I'll be fine."

CHAPTER 17

The only thing to fear is fear itself, Ava told herself as she climbed the stairs in DR's building… *that and unknown intruders.*

Falling off the ladder yesterday had disturbed her more than she would admit. She hadn't died like DR, but she could have seriously hurt herself.

Ava unlocked the door to DR's apartment and walked around it, ready to flee if she saw someone.

No one was there. Nor were there any dead bodies.

While finding dead bodies was part and parcel of being a sleuth, it was the aspect of the profession that Ava disliked the most.

What she found exciting was the chase… figuring out what was going on and who did or didn't do it. However, in the present case, she had no idea what was going on or the slightest inkling as to who might have done it.

Pulling her shoulders back, she took a deep breath. It was time to get back in the saddle. In this case, the saddle was DR's books.

Before she did that, she walked back to the still open door and inspected the doorframe for any scratches or marks indicating that someone had forced the door.

There were none.

Whoever had been in the apartment yesterday had a key.

Still not entirely at ease, Ava closed the door behind her. She noticed that she had to push hard for it to close.

Immediately, Ava felt better.

The mystery was solved.

Aymeric's story of finding the door was very possible.

Delighted to be making progress in the case, Ava locked the door. She also positioned a chair in front of it and texted Henri that she was at DR's and would text him when she left.

Better safe than sorry.

Although as Henri was in Switzerland, she didn't know how he could help her.

With a sigh, Ava eyed the bookshelves. It was time to get to work. She walked over to a shelf, took several books off it and carried them to the round table. She pulled a high backed chair up to the table and set to work.

Cataloguing books could be an almost meditative process… But after two hours, Ava was antsy and frustrated. She hadn't found any hidden messages, secret writing or any valuable books. Narrowing her eyes, she looked at the bookshelves. There were thousands of books there. A clue might be hidden in any one of them... or not.

It was too early to declare defeat.

She went to the kitchen and made herself a coffee using DR's fancy espresso machine.

Coffee in hand, Ava walked back into the living room and looked around in full-sleuth mode.

What had DR hidden, and where had he hidden it?

The most obvious thing he could have hidden was information about a secret bank account. DR had told Garance that he had the money to open his foundation. And then he didn't…

Where was the money?

Had someone stolen it and killed DR when he discovered the theft?

On the other hand, what was going on might have nothing to do with money.

Jean Colbert had spoken about fake wine. Could DR have discovered proof of this? Was he killed to stop him from talking?

At a loss for answers, Ava walked over to the bookcase, stood on her toes, gathered more books and carried them to the table.

Sitting down, she opened the first book and froze.

Something on the floor caught her eye.

Cautiously, she stood up and walked over to a tiny piece of blue and white cloth on the rug near the desk.

She leaned over and picked it up.

It was a linen handkerchief.

The initials FC were embroidered on it.

FC… François Croix.

Feeling weak in the knees, Ava sank to the ground. She should have seen the handkerchief immediately. But she hadn't… Had it been there the day before?

She turned the handkerchief over and over in her hand.

This was either a major breakthrough or someone was trying to frame François.

In either case, she was certain that the handkerchief hadn't been there when she and Henri had come for lunch. Henri would have noticed it. That's the way he was.

Unsettled by her discovery, Ava felt a sudden urge to leave the apartment. She grabbed her belongings, slid the handkerchief inside her handbag and walked to the door. She pushed the chair aside, unlocked the door, slammed it tightly shut behind her, locked it and then ran for dear life down the stairs.

When she reached the street, Ava took a deep breath and sent Henri a short text message:

Handkerchief with initials FC found at DR's.

Her head spinning, Ava walked to the funicular, waited in line and took it down the butte. As it neared the bottom, a text message from Henri popped on her phone:

Message received! New developments here. Breakfast 9:30 tomorrow.

A burst of excitement rushed through Ava.

Henri had learned something!

Perhaps it would explain why François Croix had gone to DR's apartment or someone wanted them to think that...

Buoyed, Ava exited the funicular and stepped into the crowd just as a familiar figure went past.

She blinked in disbelief.

It was Lee Baresi.

Taking this as a sign from the heavens, Ava ducked into the crowd and followed Lee down the street. In no hurry, he walked at a leisurely pace. This forced Ava to slow down even more, causing her to bump into people. At the Marché St. Pierre, Lee turned left and made his way to the French Corkscrew. When he reached it, he tried the door. It was locked.

Frowning, Lee peered through the window.

Ava inched forward to see more. A woman's reflection stared back at her from the glass window next to Lee.

It was her reflection.

CHAPTER 18

In horror, Ava stared at her reflection in the window of the French Corkscrew. When Lee Baresi turned, Ava smiled her most innocent smile and stepped toward him. To her astonishment, he wheeled around and strode off in the direction he had just come from, adjusting his ear buds.

Ava let out a deep sigh.

She was in luck again!

Lee hadn't seen her reflection.

Like a bloodhound, she trailed behind Lee, keeping him in sight at all times. At first, she lagged far behind. But when he neared the funicular station and the crowd grew denser, Ava picked up her pace, worried that she might lose him. When he got in line to take the funicular up to the top, she ducked behind the flower kiosk and waited.

Peering out from behind some long stemmed roses, she thought of taking the same car up with him, but decided against it. She wanted to see where he was going. Did he intend to search DR's place? Did he have the keys? She'd never find out if she went up in the same car with him.

Ava eyed the line. Compared to earlier, it was mercifully short. That meant as soon as Lee took a car up, she would be able to take the next one. There was a five or six minute lag between each car. If he were to run off, she'd lose him. But if he walked at a normal pace, she'd be able to catch him.

The silver funicular car glided down the rail and came to a silent halt in front of the platform. It opened its doors and the car emptied out. Immediately, the people in line pushed their way into the car. Lee disappeared inside with them. When the silver doors closed, the car began to glide up the hill.

When the next car approached, Ava sprang into action. Pointing to a man at the front of the line, she elbowed her way through the crowd. "Excuse me! Excuse me! My husband is up there."

Grumbling, people let her go by.

She reached the man just as the next car opened its doors. Ava pushed past him, stepped inside and positioned herself next to the door to be the first person out.

The crowd on the base of Sacré-Coeur was dense. Street musicians played as children ran around them dancing. Ava scanned the mass of humanity. There was no sign of Lee.

Had she lost him?

Trying to quell her growing panic, she moved through the crowd looking for the slender man.

He couldn't have gotten far.

Just then, a school group walked off following their teacher. Through the opening in the crowd, Ava saw Lee going up a street to her left in the opposite direction of DR's apartment.

In a flash, Ava began to run, shouting, "Lee… Lee!"

Lee didn't slow. In fact, he appeared to walk faster.

"Lee!" Ava shouted again as she stopped to adjust the strap on her sandals.

When he halted to look out over the city, Ava sprinted toward him. Reaching him, she tapped him on the shoulder.

Startled, he turned to her.

For a brief instant, he didn't recognize her. Then he smiled and took his ear buds out of his ears. "Ava? The book lady?"

"The very same," Ava replied, catching her breath.

"What are you doing up here?" Lee asked.

"I was at DR's cataloguing books… But it's too beautiful to work. I'm playing hooky," Ava confessed.

Lee nodded in agreement. "It is too beautiful to work. If DR were alive, he'd be opening a special bottle to celebrate the good weather. He opened special bottles to celebrate the smallest things. He believed that's what wine was for."

"What are you doing up here?" Ava asked, trying not to

appear too interested.

"I wanted to see DR's shop again. But it was closed. I should have expected that. As it's beautiful, I decided to visit my favorite place in the whole world. If you have time, I'll show you..." Lee said with an easy smile.

Ava jumped at the chance to spend more time with him. "I'd love to see it. Is it far?"

"Far? A ten or fifteen minute walk." He eyed her sandals. "You'll make it with no problem."

The two started up the sloping street. Lee gazed around at the old houses and greenery.

"DR loved this neighborhood."

"I have your tasting notebook," Ava blurted out impulsively.

Lee stopped walking and stared at her, astonished. "I didn't know that I'd lost it... How did you know it was mine?"

Because you wrote, "*who did it?*" on one of the pages," Ava responded as she kept her eyes on his face. As she suspected, his expression changed. She could see he was debating whether to lie to her or not.

Instead, Lee ignored her remark and began to walk. "Then I must have your notebook."

"Someone pushed Marc Virgile into traffic last night." Again, Ava didn't know why she told Lee that, but her words had an immediate effect on the man.

"Oh my God! How is he?" Lee asked in shock. "Was he hurt?"

"Physically, he's fine. For the rest, he's as ornery as usual. But I think he's more shaken than he'd like to admit. Only Henri and I know about his accident," Ava added.

Shifting his weight from foot to foot, Lee stared at her. "Why are you telling me this?"

"Because I want to know who did it," Ava replied. "Just like you."

Lee didn't answer her. Tight-lipped, he strode off. Ava walked next to him. When they reached the *Clos de Montmartre*, a tiny vineyard owned by the city of Paris, Lee halted and peered through the iron fence at the vines that were growing inside. He had a nostalgic expression on his face.

"This is why I went into wine," Lee said truly moved by the vineyard. He pointed to a tall building on the other side of the *Clos de Montmartre*. "When I was a child, my father worked at a big brokerage house in Paris. We lived in that building. From my bedroom window, I watched the grapes grow. One year, I even helped with the harvest. The workers told me that wine was magical. I believed them."

"Do you still believe them?" Ava asked, surprised by his remark.

Lee grinned. "Even more so. Wine is so magical that people pay small fortunes for certain bottles. I'm not complaining. Money makes the world go round. But I still come here when I want to remember the awe I felt as a child." Lee pointed at a bistro up the hill. "Let's sit down so we can talk. But I warn you, I don't know anything about Marc Virgile's accident."

The bistro was on the side of a steep street with no traffic. With the vineyard nearby and birds chirping in a garden across the way, it was like being in the countryside. Lee chose a table on the outside terrace. He opened the wine menu and studied it.

"Do you have a preference?" Lee asked looking up at Ava.

"No. Order for both of us."

When the waiter arrived, Lee pointed to a wine on the menu. The waiter wrote it down and left.

Lee sat back in his chair. "It's an inexpensive wine from Bordeaux. You won't be disappointed. It's a far cry from a Domaine de Kirjac. But it's a perfect wine for a summer afternoon."

When the waiter brought the wine, he poured it in Lee's glass. Lee sniffed, swirled, and took a sip. A smile spread across his face. He nodded at the waiter who poured wine in Ava's glass and set the bottle on the table. Ava sipped her wine. Lee hadn't lied. It was perfect for a summer afternoon.

Silent, Lee stared at her before speaking, "Before I answer your questions, I want you to answer one for me. Was DR's death an accident?"

"I don't know. Why would it be?" Ava replied.

Lee shrugged. "Because of what Marc Virgile said at the tasting… that DR suspected that one of us was trying to kill him. And now someone has pushed Marc into traffic… Unless Marc lied to draw suspicion away from himself."

Ava was so startled by Lee's words that she put her wine glass down on the table. *Was that possible? Was this all a set up by Marc Virgile?*

Lee sipped his wine. "I was being disingenuous when I said at the tasting that I didn't know why DR invited me. I know why. We both deal with very wealthy buyers…the top 10%. My buyers are younger and more international than DR's. But they both want the same impossible to find wines. DR was good at finding those wines. Often, I'd sell his wines to my clients and split the commission."

"Where did the money go?" Ava asked

"DR had an account in Singapore. But money wasn't his primary motive. I won't deny that he loved the glitter and glamour of selling high-end wines. The private jets. The yachts. The dinners in high-priced restaurants… But most of all, he loved wine. That's why he kept his shop after he stopped selling wine there. It was his private paradise."

"Was he selling fake wine?" Ava asked.

Lee raised his eyebrows, outraged. "Of course not. That doesn't mean he didn't sell some fake bottles. Who hasn't? How would you even know? DR always made it clear to his customers that if they weren't 100% confident in what he sold, he'd buy it back. That just made his buyers more willing to deal with him."

"Wasn't there a problem with the Domaine de Kirjac last year?" Ava asked.

Lee nodded. "Marc Virgile's nephew made a big deal about a case of wine that he thought was fake. He was wrong. Luckily, Marc nipped it in the bud. But DR was concerned as he was the one who had put the wine up for auction. He'd spent years getting to where he was. He didn't want it to come crashing down. Rumors, even false rumors, have consequences."

"Did you see him before he died?" Ava asked.

Lee nodded. "We all did. Everyone at the tasting was in Paris that week for a big wine auction. I had dinner with DR the night before he died in Montmartre. He was angry about the fake wine accusation. He was even angrier that he couldn't actively defend himself as that would confirm there was a problem. I told him to relax. Things would die down."

"And did they?"

"Yes. But now I have a problem," Lee said as he poured each of them more wine. "One of my best clients suspects he bought fake wine through DR."

"What's he going to do about it?" Ava asked.

Lee reared his head back, astonished. "He wants me to find out if it's true and who is responsible for it. You just don't open a bottle of wine that cost 10,000 euros a bottle to check if you were cheated, even if you are a millionaire. In fact, he doesn't want to open it. The wine is an investment. In another ten years, the wine will be worth 30,000 euros a bottle."

Hearing the figure, Ava's eyes popped out of her head. "How is that possible?"

"Scarcity… There are only so many bottles of a Cheval Blanc, a Chateau Margaux or a Domaine de Kirjac. Hence the price," Lee explained. "If the wine is fake which I don't know it is… someone knows about it. That's why I wrote "who did it?" in my notebook. Everyone there was linked to DR's last big wine sale."

"I don't understand," Ava said. "Everyone where? At the tasting?"

Lee nodded. "François Croix had sold DR wine from his cellar. Old bottles. Impossible to find bottles. The fact that he was the seller was a secret."

Ava narrowed her eyes. "You found out?"

"That's why I'm good at what I do. I need to learn who is selling and who is buying. I suspect Marc Virgile used DR to sell wine. For certain years, there were more bottles of Domaine de Kirjac available than people knew. By selling through DR in private sales, Marc was able to keep his prices high. Roger Allard also sold wine through DR."

"And Diane de la Floch?" Ava asked, wondering where the woman fit into the scheme of things.

Lee shrugged. "I know she bought wine from DR. Did she sell wine through him? I can't tell you that."

Ava eyed Lee. "DR believed that one of you at the tasting had tried to kill him. Why were you on the list?"

"No! Maybe he thought I was cheating him. I wasn't…" Lee replied.

"How are you going to discover who is behind the fake wine?" Ava asked.

Lee let out a long sigh. "I can't. But I'm buying time. If I obtain the wine from Marc Virgile on Saturday, I'll sell it to that client. He will be more than happy to forget everything if that's the price he has to pay to get Marc's wine."

Deep in thought, Ava tilted her head to the side. "Who is your client?"

Lee smiled. "That's a trade secret. DR also intended to have it out with Marc's nephew. Marc convinced him not to. Marc said he'd deal with his nephew in his own way."

Ava thought back to Aymeric's timely appearance at DR's apartment. Could Aymeric be behind his uncle's accident? If he could convince his uncle his life was in danger, maybe Marc would deal with Aymeric's suspicions of fake Domaine de Kirjac being sold differently. Ava sighed. It was all so complicated.

Lee eyed her and seemed to read her thoughts. "It's not an easy situation. I'm having dinner with Diane tonight."

Ava raised her eyebrows. "Why?"

"I suspect she wants to work together to get the wine. Better 50% than zero… that sort of thinking," Lee said.

"And?" Ava asked.

"I don't operate that way… But there's no one else she can ask. Diane doesn't get along with Roger Allard. Roger is a firm believer that women don't belong in the wine world. Diane hates François. She'd do anything to bring him down. If she knew that François and Solange had a fling, she'd be furious."

Ava couldn't believe her ears. "François and Solange had a fling? How do you know that?"

"DR and I saw them together."

"When?" Ava asked, trying to imagine the two together.

"The night before DR died. He and I were leaving the restaurant when they went by all lovey dovey. They didn't see us."

"What was DR's reaction?" Ava asked.

"He was angry with Solange. Not because she was seeing François, but because she hadn't told him. If DR was killed, Solange didn't do it. They adored each other."

"And François?" Ava asked.

Lee burst out laughing. "If François had killed DR, he would have left so many clues that the police would have caught him. He's a notorious bumbler."

CHAPTER 19

Solange and François… François and Solange… Ava tried to wrap her mind around the idea that the two had had some kind of relationship. At the tasting, they had barely looked at one another.

Was it really possible that they had dated?

Perhaps Lee and DR misinterpreted what they saw. After all, Lee said that they had had only glimpsed the two briefly.

To Ava, François and Solange were an improbable couple. François was a total snob while Solange was warm and down to earth. If the two had had a brief fling that might explain Solange's praise for François in her book. And if they had broken up afterwards, that would explain Solange's bad-mouthing François yesterday.

Hadn't Pascal, the French philosopher, said that the heart has reasons that reason doesn't understand?

Even if the two had the worst breakup in the world that didn't make either of them a murderer. However, François's reputation for being a bumbler increased the chances that he had been the one who had dropped the handkerchief at DR's.

If it was him, what was he looking for? If it wasn't him, why was someone trying to frame him?

At an impasse, Ava sighed and looked out the window as her taxi sped down toward the Seine. When it reached the Quai Malaquais, Ava paid the driver and climbed out. Her stand was shuttered as was Ali's. A voice shouted out her name. Puzzled, she spun around. Alain, the chef and co-owner of Café Zola, was waving at her from the café doorway.

Seated in the back of the café, Ava smiled as Alain, a tall, thin man in his thirties, lined up wine glasses before them.

For Ava, Alain was more than a chef. He was an alchemist who could take the simplest ingredients and produce perfection. He was also her food guru who had changed her relationship with food forever.

The first time she had eaten at the café with Henri, she had ordered a sandwich. Alain was so upset that he had come out of the kitchen to see what was wrong. The sandwich was replaced by a *coq au vin*, rooster in wine sauce, and a *tarte tatin*, a caramelized upside down apple tart, for dessert. It was delicious. It was also life changing. Ava had never looked back.

"You came by at the right time. I'm tasting the reds in

our fall line-up," Alain said as he picked up a bottle of wine and poured some for each of them.

Ava watched the red liquid gently fill into her glass. Suddenly, her whole life was centered on wine.

He then poured thre more reds out. "A Bordeaux, a Bergerac and a wine from Corsica."

Ava tasted them. "They're all great… really great." Feeling a presence next to her, she looked up.

Gerard, Alain's cousin, was staring down at her with mock pity. "Ava, you're in France. You have to up your wine game. "Great" doesn't cut the cake…"

Alain shook his head. "Don't traumatize her, Gerard."

Ava sat up straight. "I'm not traumatized. At least, not yet…" The young woman eyed Gerard. "Please continue."

Gerard nodded. "Wine 101… A beginner's guide on how to fake it." He picked up a wine glass by its stem. "First, pick up the glass and swirl it to release the aroma components. You then tip the glass slightly. Study the color of the wine as if you were looking for hidden treasure."

Grinning, Alain jumped into the game. "You can then swirl again if you'd like."

Ava picked up her glass of red wine, swirled, tipped it, stared into it, swirled it gently again and nodded.

"I like the nod. That's good improv," Gerard said with approval.

"You've got a knack for this, Ava," Alain teased.

Ava shook her head and looked at both men. "Now I am traumatized."

Gerard brought the glass to his nose. "Sniff gently. You can talk about the "nose" of the wine."

"Rich or lovely… Keep it simple," Alain added.

Ava sniffed her wine. "The nose is rich."

"Now take a small sip and savor it. At an industry wine tasting, you'll be spitting it out. But in other cases, you swallow what you've just drunk," Gerard explained.

Ava sipped her wine and swallowed.

Gerard smiled. "Now comes the trickiest part. Let someone else give their opinion first."

"Then agree!" Alain said. He picked up a glass of wine and sipped it. "Generous with ripe tannins…"

"And a beautiful intensity," Ava added, parroting what Diane had said at the tasting

"You've got it. You have now graduated from wine 101," Gerard said before striding away.

"I swear he gets worse every year," Alain said as his cousin walked off.

"His bark is worse than his bite," Ava said. "French waiters have a reputation for being testy. Gerard is just living up to the hype."

Alain sat down and filled two glasses to the top. "The tasting is officially over. It's time to drink some wine."

Ava tipped her glass, studied the color and then sipped it.

"It's great, isn't it?" Alain said.

"I won't respond to that," Ava said as she enjoyed the wine. Her mind went back to her conversation with Lee. "Is there a lot of fraud in wine?"

"In any sector, if there's money to be made, there's fraud. Not just in wine. As a chef, I have to be wary of fish fraud. Sole that isn't sole. Caviar that isn't caviar. Alaskan salmon that isn't from Alaska. The list goes on and on. With DNA testing, it's become easier to uncover fraud."

"You can do a DNA test on fish?" Ava asked, startled.

Alain nodded. "Absolutely. Fraud is everywhere. When I was a child, we went to a petting zoo each summer. It was obvious that the zebra was a donkey that had been painted. I didn't say anything as I didn't want to hurt its feelings. Does this have to do with your new case?"

Ava's eyes widened. "You know about it?"

Alain shook his head. "I guessed. Henri had a wedding in Bordeaux. He didn't go to Bordeaux. There's only one thing that would keep him here… a case."

"We went to a tasting of Domaine de Kirjac."

Alain whistled and looked at her admiringly. "You're starting at the top. I've only tasted Domaine de Kirjac once.

It was unforgettable." Alain eyed Ava, worried. "You didn't say "great"?"

"No. I didn't say anything. I wish I'd had Gerard's course before the tasting."

Alain shouted at Gerard, "Bring us something to nibble on."

At the bar, Gerard sighed like a martyr and headed to the kitchen.

"Who does the case center on?" Alain asked.

"One dead man, David Rose, known as DR, who was either murdered or not. He dealt in high-end wines all over the world. One important wine broker from Burgundy."

"Roger Allard?" Alain asked with a serious look on his face.

Ava was startled. "How did you guess?"

"Roger Allard is "the" wine broker in Burgundy. He's a rainmaker. If he buys your little known wine, you're on your way. He's tough as nails. I wouldn't want to tangle with him."

Gerard brought over a basket of bread and some sausage on a wooden cutting board.

"Diane de la Floch…" Ava added.

"Wasn't she married to a billionaire?" Gerard asked.

Ava eyed him. "How do you know that?"

"Her divorce was a major scandal. Her husband tried to

run her over with his Jaguar. It was in all the Parisian papers," Gerard said and walked off.

"Who else?" Alain asked as he took a piece of bread.

"Diane's cousin who took over the family vineyard, François Croix."

Alain put a piece of sausage on the bread and took a bite. "I've never heard of him."

"Marc Virgile, owner of Domaine de Kirjac. Lee Baresi, an Asian New Yorker who grew up in Paris who deals in high-end wine. There's also Solange Vitrang who wrote a book on the history of Burgundy wine."

" I read it. It was very scholarly… perhaps overly so." Alain pushed the sausage to Ava. "So you think there might be fake wine?"

"It's a possibility."

Alain shook his head. "You'll never find out if it's true or not…"

"Why do you say that?" Ava asked, surprised.

"Because everyone in the wine world will close ranks. No one wants a scandal."

Ava looked troubled. "Then someone wouldn't kill because of it?"

"Unless the dead person was going to go to the press, I can't imagine that someone would. Especially with the type of people you said were involved. But wine means different things to different people. Today, anyone can buy a plane or a yacht if they have the money. But to buy certain rare bottles, you need more than money. You have to cultivate relationships and be lucky."

"What if the bottles were fake?"

"Why would a wealthy person tell the world they were cheated? It would make them look stupid. Most people would just shut up. That doesn't mean that money isn't behind it…"

"Or love?" Ava asked, thinking of Solange and François.

"Or both," Alain said, echoing Henri's refrain. "I leave it to you and Henri to discover which one it is."

CHAPTER 20

"You could call it "The Case of the Dropped Handkerchief," Nate said on the other end of the line.

Ava shifted on the couch in the moonlight as a scented candle flickered on the coffee table next to her. A glass of red wine was in her hand. She took a sip and spoke, "We don't know that François dropped it. We don't even know that it belongs to him."

"Unless there was another FC at the tasting, everything points to François."

"That's just too easy. You need a twist in a crime case," Ava protested.

"Ava, this is real life. You don't need a twist," Nate said, unable to hide his amusement.

"I disagree. Even in real life -- especially in real life -- things can be more complicated than they seem. The handkerchief might have fallen out of François's pocket, but it could also have been placed there by someone else."

"Is there some reason you don't want François to have

dropped it?" Nate asked.

"You would think I would want him to have dropped it. Out of all of the people at the tasting, François is the one I liked the least."

"What did he do to offend you?"

"Nothing specific. He had an air of entitlement about him. Lee said he was a *fils de papa,* someone who got where his is because of his father's money and clout," Ava explained.

"A lot of men owe their success to their families but that doesn't mean that they go around willy-nilly breaking into apartments and scaring people off ladders."

"It doesn't mean that they don't." Annoyed, Ava stopped. Nate had done it again. He had her arguing against her own theory -- that it wasn't really Francois who had broken into the apartment. "I'm always suspicious of an easy solution. It makes me feel that I'm missing something. Lee said François was a bumbler who would have left tons of clues if he killed DR. So maybe it was François who scared me. A handkerchief is a fairly obvious clue."

"You're mixing apples and oranges. François could be the one who dropped the handkerchief but not the one who scared you!"

"I'm going to put this piece of evidence in the "wait and see" category," Ava said with a sigh. She had been so happy to discover a clue and now her clue had muddied the waters.

"You know what Freud said?" Nate asked.

Ava took a sip of wine, waiting for him to continue.

"Sometimes a cigar is just a cigar."

Ava frowned, puzzled. "So a handkerchief is just a handkerchief. And that means?"

"That you're giving the handkerchief a lot of importance... and it might not be that important."

"You mean that the handkerchief could be a red herring put there to throw me off the track?" Ava asked.

"Exactly. Now tell me about Lee."

"He's smart, cultivated, handsome and has a poetic soul."

Nate snorted in indignation. "Now I'm jealous."

Ava burst out laughing. "Nothing could shake your self-confidence. You are utterly certain that every woman on the planet adores you."

"I only care about one woman. And I know you adore me. Why wouldn't you?" Nate teased.

"See what I mean," Ava replied with a grin. "Lee spoke about fake wine. When I tasted wine at Café Zola today, Alain told me that there are fakes of everything. Fake salmon. Fake caviar. Fake cheese. Fake organic food."

"The products are real."

"But they don't match the name. When I buy an organic free-range chicken, I don't expect a battery chicken raised in a cramped cage," Ava said.

"Next you'll be asking for the chicken's college diploma and three character references..."

"You're not taking this seriously."

"I assure you I am. What does Lee hope to find?"

"Nothing. He's just buying time. How could he find out who's behind the fake wine... if the wine is fake. That remains to be seen. He's a wine broker, not a detective."

"You could help him," Nate suggested.

"Henri and I already have one case. That's enough for this week." Suddenly, Ava's eye opened wide. "I forgot to tell you the most important thing... Lee and DR saw François and Solange together. They suspected the two were seeing each other."

"That wouldn't surprise me."

"What?" Ava responded, as her mouth fell open in astonishment.

"Ava, you're far too Anglo-Saxon in your approach to sex. François is a playboy. Solange was there to write about his winery. You told me that she's beautiful and single. It goes with the territory."

"That's a sexist remark."

"Ask Henri." When Ava didn't answer him, Nate sighed. "At least, think about it."

Ava was thinking about it. When Lee had told her about seeing the pair together, she had hoped that the men were mistaken. *Why?* For the simple reason that she liked Solange and didn't like François. Plus, she didn't want to buy into the stereotype of the beautiful woman and the wealthy cheating husband.

"What's your next move?" Nate asked.

"I'm having breakfast with Henri tomorrow to see what he learned in Geneva. Tomorrow is Friday, if we don't discover something soon, the wine sale will be over and so will our case. On Saturday, everyone will be at Marc's dinner. If Henri and I have more information, we can confront the suspect."

"If I'm not mistaken, that usually leads to another murder."

"As you said, this is real life, not an Agatha Christie mystery. I also want to have another go at Solange, woman to woman. And maybe have another look around DR's apartment. Someone is searching for something. It might be hidden there. I'd also like to check out the wine shop. Something there caught Lee's attention."

"It sounds like you and Henri will have a long day tomorrow."

"Sleuthing is not a 9-5 job." Ava changed the subject. "Enough of me. Tell me about your film."

"The truck delivering the film reels was hijacked. We've had to rush more film stock from the UK. One of the actresses saw a mouse in her trailer and had a panic attack. We broke the door down to get her to the set. And it rained, and we were shooting a sunny day scene. All in all, things are going well."

"You're joking?" Ava asked.

"I wish I were. It's a typical day in the life of a film," Nate said fatalistic.

"Your life would be less eventful if you were a sleuth."

Nate chuckled. "I'll leave the sleuthing to you. How's Mercury?"

"He popped in after you left, but vanished again. The food was still in his bowl when I came home this evening. He's probably off to the south of France for a long weekend."

"You're jealous that he likes me," Nate replied.

Ava shifted on the couch. "No… I'm worried that the only reason you're with me is to worm your way into Mercury's life."

Nate laughed. "Mercury's a harder nut to crack than you think. And with that, I'm going to bed. I have to get up at 4 am. Who knows what wonders await me tomorrow?"

Ava hung up and poured herself more wine. Her mind went back to Lee's comment about wanting to go to the shop again. What was it that had drawn his attention? All she remembered was wine. She needed to get into the shop before the tasting.. She suspected that was easier said than done.

CHAPTER 21

"*Pain au chocolat* or a croissant?" Henri asked as he opened a bag from the bakery… not just any bakery, but the best bakery in Paris.

Ava knew exactly what she wanted. "Both," she said without shame.

Henri looked up at her, surprised.

"Sleuthing burns calories!" Ava replied, non-apologetic.

Henri put a pain au chocolat and a croissant on a paper plate and handed it to her. He served himself a pain au chocolat while Ava poured coffee from a thermos into their cups.

They were sitting on the edge of the Seine on the right bank. They could see their stands across the river. They also had a view of the *Square du Vert Galant*, the tiny piece of land at the end of the Ile de la Cité that was linked to the Templars. Ava's legs dangled over the water as swans floated by. Overhead, the long wisplike branches of a weeping willow blew in the wind. It was an idyllic scene. It was a perfect spot to have breakfast and discuss the case.

"Who goes first?" Henri asked, sipping his coffee. Always chic, he was dressed in dark grey cotton trousers and a pale blue shirt.

Looking at him, Ava was glad that she had won a stylish blue skirt and a crisp white T-shirt. On her feet, she was wearing navy blue espadrilles that she had bought at a street market in Nice. "You," Ava said, anxious to hear what Henri had learned.

Henri nodded. "Garance called me from Singapore. She was finally able to get into DR's accounts. They were almost empty.

"The money's vanished?" Ava asked, alarmed.

Henri shook his head. "Not exactly. Eighteen months ago, DR transferred three million euros to a holding company in Lichtenstein. The trail stops there."

Ava face showed her disappointment. She bit into her pain au chocolat. The pastry melted in her mouth. She regretted not asking for two.

"However, my notary friend that I met in Geneva told me about parcel of land – wine growing land -- that was bought by the same holding company in Lichtenstein for almost the same amount that was transferred out of the accounts."

Ava looked up, silent. She could tell from the tone of Henri's voice that he had learned much more than that.

"Rumor has it that Marc Virgile was involved," Henri announced.

Ava was startled. "It's not just a rumor?"

Henri shook his head as if to say he didn't deal in rumors. "My friend is certain… "

"What happened to the parcel of land?" Ava asked.

"It's funny you ask. The land was sold a month ago to another holding. Again, Marc Virgile was rumored to be the person selling."

Ava stopped eating and fell silent. "Did Marc kill DR to get the money?"

Henri shook his head. "That's hard to believe. I wish Marc had told us what's going on."

"Maybe that's why someone pushed him into traffic… " Ava said as her mind began racing. Immediately, Aymeric jumped to the top of her suspect list. Did he know about the money?

"Marc warned us that someone might have reasons to kill him. I didn't believe him. I thought he was being dramatic," Henri said. "I was wrong."

"It might have been a warning. Give us the money or you'll die…" Ava suggested as she poured herself more coffee.

Henri bit into his pain au chocolat. "But if he died, how would they get the money…"

"Inheritance!" Ava said feeling disloyal. She liked Aymeric and didn't want to believe that he was behind his uncle's accident. But so far, he had the best motive.

Henri knitted his eyebrows together in thought. "Perhaps. However, I can't see Aymeric pushing his uncle into traffic. What puzzles me is why DR emptied his account to buy a parcel of land. It wasn't what he did, and it tied up all his money."

"Someone might have blackmailed him into doing it," Ava suggested.

"That doesn't make sense. Marc Virgile is involved in the holding. From what we know, the men were friends until the end. There is something going on that I don't understand."

"Did Garance learn anything else?" Ava asked.

"She has one last meeting this morning before she flies back." Henri broke off a piece of his pain au chocolat and threw it in the water. A swan swam over, lowered its neck and gobbled it down.

"Did your notary friend have anything to say about the others?" Ava asked.

"Unsurprisingly, he doesn't think much of François Croix. He confirmed that François's wife has left him, and they are getting a divorce."

"She's wealthy. Will he get a lot of money?" Ava asked.

"They married under the separation of property regime. He won't get a cent from her. She might give him some money to have peace. After all, she's been paying for everything for years."

Ava wrinkled her nose, puzzled. "Doesn't he earn money

from running the winery?"

"Not enough to pay for his expensive tastes, including frequent gambling trips to Macao," Henri replied.

"What did your friend say about Diane?" Ava asked, curious to hear an insider's view of the woman.

"She's rich, smart, and knows how to get what she wants. She's a ruthless competitor in every way…"

"And she hates François…" Ava added. "His goose is cooked." In a duel between the two, there could only be one outcome.

"Can I see the famous handkerchief?" Henri asked.

Proud as punch, Ava removed it from her handbag and handed it to him.

He turned it over in his hand and studied the FC embroidered on it. "Did he lose it or did someone else put it there?"

"I have no idea but Lee Baresi said that François was a bumbler. He even said that it was impossible that François had anything to do with DR's death because he would have left a trail of clues leading back to him."

Henri looked amused. "He's that bad?"

Ava nodded. "Lee believes so. He had dinner with DR the night before he died. They saw François and Solange walking arm and arm. DR was angry that Solange hadn't told him about the relationship."

"I'm not surprised they were dating."

Ava's eyes opened wide. "What? Nate told me that you'd say that."

"François fancies himself a playboy. Solange is a beautiful woman who wrote flattering things about him in her book. I assumed there was a reason for that."

"Does that make them suspects?"

Henri shook his head. "Unless we get more information that points toward them, I don't think so. Tell me more about Lee. Where did you meet him?"

"Right after I texted you about the handkerchief, I took the funicular down to the bottom of the butte. When I got off, Lee was walking by. I followed him to the French Corkscrew, which was closed. Then I tailed him to the top of the butte."

"Why didn't you speak to him immediately?" Henri asked.

"I wanted to see if he was meeting someone or going to DR's."

"And did he go there?" Henri asked.

Ava shook her head. "No. He didn't meet anyone either. I pretended to run into him near Sacré-Coeur. He went up to see the *Clos de Montmartre*. He lived behind the vineyard as a child. It's a yearly pilgrimage for him. It reminds him that wine is magical."

Henri smiled approvingly. "I like that. It gives him

character. What else did you learn?"

"I have his tasting notebook."

"He admitted it was his?" Henri asked, astonished.

"I cornered him into confessing. I also told him about Marc's accident."

"What was his reaction?

"Shock." Ava bit into her croissant. It was delicious but not as tasty as the pain au chocolat.

"He also has a big problem. One of his uber wealthy clients believes he bought fake wine through DR. He asked Lee to discover who's behind it."

"And the possibilities are?"

"Marc Virgile, DR, or Roger Allard. Or someone else who sold it to them – so perhaps François."

Henri was silent. "What does Lee intend to do?"

"Buy time. He doesn't believe he'll discover who is behind it if the wine is fake. But if he gets Marc's wine that will smooth things over."

Suddenly, Ava's phone beeped. It was a text message. She read it and looked up at Henri. "Solange wants to have lunch with me. She says it's important."

"Does she say anything more than that?" Henri asked.

Ava shook her head. "What are your plans today?"

"I'm seeing someone else who knows Roger and Marc. Time is running out. Marc's dinner is tomorrow. If we don't find out more, something bad is going to happen."

Ava had a sinking feeling in her stomach. How would they ever discover what they needed to know in twenty-four hours?

"I'm also going to look into Aymeric and see if I can't learn more about Marc's involvement with the land sale last month."

"If the money is gone, why is someone searching DR's apartment for it?" Ava asked.

"Either the person doesn't know the money is gone or they are looking for something entirely different. There might even be two people looking for different things."

Ava frowned. "Which means that the person who killed DR -- if DR was killed -- might not be the person who pushed Marc into traffic."

"Or the person who frightened you..." Henri finished his coffee and packed the cups and thermos into a carrying bag. He stood up and dusted himself off. "How's Nate?"

"The truck delivering the film was hijacked. The main actress locked herself in her dressing room and refused to come out. And they had torrential rain all day for an exterior shoot that was supposed to take place on a sunny day," Ava said with a grin.

"Nate would have a quieter life as a sleuth."

"One sleuth in our couple is enough," Ava protested as she brushed the crumbs off her skirt.

"When you talk to Solange, try and find out more about Marc. She might have had more interaction with him than she said."

Ava raised her eyebrows. "And Francois?"

"Hell hath no fury like a woman scorned…" Henri said.

"Or a man who has been discarded," Ava replied, tick for tack.

"Or a man who has been discarded," Henri acknowledged. "I apologize for my out-dated view of the situation."

CHAPTER 22

The café was located on the rue des Abbesses, the street that ran along the bottom of the butte. As Ava cut across the square that was across from the café, she stopped in front of an old-fashioned merry-go-round and watched the brightly painted wooden horses go up and down as their young riders squealed in delight. Ava wished she were young enough to join them.

With regret, Ava left the square and crossed the street to the café. Solange was sitting at an outdoor table under a red and white striped awning. Ava was happy that the table was in the shade as the temperature was rising quickly.

Solange rose to her feet and kissed Ava on the cheeks as friends do in France.

Were they friends? Ava wondered as she sat down.

Solange was pale and tense. "Thank you for coming on such short notice."

"You said it was important."

"It is," Solange replied. "Very important."

Before Solange could say more, the waiter appeared. A jovial bearded man in his twenties, he handed each woman a menu.

"Everything here is fabulous, but I recommend the spinach and ricotta salad."

"With a drizzle of honey?" Solange asked.

The waiter grinned. "You've eaten here before." He eyed Ava. "The chef raises bees. If he can put honey on a dish, he does."

Ava closed the menu. "One ricotta and spinach salad with lots of honey. I don't raise bees. I just love honey."

Solange closed her menu "The same for me."

"Wine?" the waiter asked.

"Absolutely," Ava responded and looked at Solange. "You're the expert. You choose."

Solange studied the wine list that was written on a slate hanging from the wall. "A carafe of the house Chablis."

When the waiter left, Ava sat back in her chair and waited for the other woman to speak.

Ill at ease, Solange cleared her throat. "I received a threat."

Alarmed, Ava caught her breath. "From who?"

Solange swallowed. "I don't know. Someone called me yesterday evening. No number. I answered. The person said,

"Find DR's money or you'll end up like him."

Ava was stunned.

"I was so shocked I didn't know what to do," Solange said wringing her hands together. "I stood there looking at my phone for an eternity."

"Did you recognize the voice?"

Solange shook her head. "It happened so fast. Plus the voice was distorted."

Ava sighed. There were lots of apps that let you distort your voice as a prank. Solange's caller had probably used one of those.

"At first, I thought it was a joke. I don't have DR's money or have any idea where it is. If I did, I'd be leading the high life or planning to. Instead, I'm taking an inventory of his wines. A very poor selection in my opinion."

"Why would someone believe you know where his money is?" Ava asked.

"DR often joked to people that I'd be a rich widow. He had an odd sense of humor. Maybe someone believed him."

Ava kept her eyes on Solange's face. "Who do you think it was?"

"I suppose it was someone from the tasting. But that makes no sense."

"Why?" Ava asked. If she had to draw up a list of suspects, the people at the tasting would be at the top of her list.

"Because no one there needs money, and they have no reason to think I have it. However, the call came the day after the tasting. So the two must be linked."

"Perhaps someone suspects you were involved with DR's death," Ava said.

Instantly, Solange raised her hand to her throat as if to ward off a fatal blow. "Involved in DR's death? That's absurd. His death devastated me. DR was my friend... my mentor. He believed in me from the start. I'm lost without him."

The waiter brought over the wine, the salads and some bread. 'Who's tasting?"

Ava pointed at Solange. "The wine expert."

The waiter poured wine in Solange's glass. She tipped her glass, swirled, sniffed, took a sip and nodded. The waiter poured more wine in her glass and then poured some for Ava. Ava sipped the wine. It was wonderful. Its acidity would compliment the honey.

Solange poked at her salad, lost in thought.

"DR had been dead over three months. You never received a call like that before?" Ava asked.

Solange shook her head. "Never!"

"Yet forty-eight hours after the tasting, someone calls you about DR's money. Diane de la Floch, for example?"

Solange knitted her eyebrows together. "If it was Diane,

it's not about money. She's rich as can be. But maybe you're right. It's not about money. It's about something else."

"Scaring you perhaps?" Ava suggested.

Solange let out a snort. "They succeeded. I didn't sleep all night." She took a bite of her salad and fell silent for a few seconds. "Diane doesn't like me, but an anonymous phone call isn't her style. She'd twist a knife in my back over and over again in public, proud of what she was doing."

"How about Roger Allard?"

Solange's expression darkened. "I don't know Roger well. He has a reputation for being cutthroat in business dealings. But why would he would threaten me? If it was someone from the tasting, I'd opt for Lee Baresi or François Croix... Why Lee? Because he's the one I know the least. He had financial dealings with DR. But then everyone there did. If you were going to buy or sell high-end impossible-to-find wines, you were bound to deal with DR at one time or another."

"How is everyone linked?" Ava asked, hoping to get a firmer grip on the relationships between the people at the tasting.

Solange ran her finger over the rim of her wine glass as she spoke. "François sold wine to DR. Roger sold wine through DR. DR advised Marc on Domaine de Kirjac. From what I saw, their relationship was more than professional. It was a true friendship. Diane bought wine from DR or used him to get wine she wanted. I know Lee often sold wine for DR, keeping the wine's origin secret."

Ava frowned. Suddenly, everything Lee had said to her yesterday seemed too easy… too confessional. Did Lee plant the handkerchief because Lee was the one who had been in the apartment? "If they all dealt with DR, why do you suspect Lee and François?"

"Because I'm sure it isn't Diane, Roger or Marc. It might be you or Henri…" Solange said as her voice trailed off.

Ava choked on her salad. "Us?"

"I don't know either of you or why Garance asked you to come to the tasting."

"I assure you neither Henri or I called you," Ava sputtered.

Solange smiled. "Of course, you didn't. I was just thinking out loud. None of this makes any sense."

"If it is about the money… Why you?" Ava asked, unsettled by Solange's strange accusation.

"I was close to DR. It wasn't always an easy friendship. DR could be awful, especially to those who cared about him. Why do I suspect Lee? The night DR died, I was supposed to have dinner with him. He called and cancelled. By chance, I saw them later that evening at a bar. They were arguing."

"About what?" Ava asked, astonished. Lee hadn't mentioned seeing DR the night he died. He'd only spoken about the night before. Could Solange be mistaken?

"I don't know what they argued about. When DR is angry, it's better to steer clear of him. That's what I did"

Ava leaned forward. "Tell me about François."

Solange's face clouded over. "There's something you need to know. I had a brief fling with him. On my side, it was a lark. But he took it very seriously. He wanted to leave his wife for me. I broke it off. We didn't see each other for months. Right before DR died, François started calling again, insisting that he couldn't live without me. I told him it was over. He wouldn't believe me. We saw each other the week before DR died as François was in Paris for the wine auction. He begged me to take him back. I refused. After the tasting the other night, against my better judgment, we had dinner. He started crying. I told him it was too late. He might have called to make me pay for my indifference."

"Where did you have dinner?" Ava asked.

"At a brasserie in Pigalle," Solange replied.

Ava said nothing. Pigalle was where Marc and Roger had eaten. There was nothing surprising that all four had dined in the same neighborhood. Pigalle was famous for its brasseries that were open around the clock. However, that put Solange and François at the same spot where Marc was pushed.

Uneasy, Solange sipped her wine. "I have a bad feeling about the tasting. It's like a joke DR is pulling from beyond the grave." A tear rolled down her cheek. "Plus, I'm worried about François. He's about to crack. His wife is leaving him. He won't have her money. And he's terrified that Diane will find out something he did."

"Did he say what that was?" Ava asked, hoping to learn more.

Solange shook her head. "He refused to tell me. François is weak. For a short time, he had the best of two worlds… me and his wife's money. Now he doesn't have me, and he'll soon lose his wife's money… and maybe the winery."

"And if he had DR's money?"

"That would change everything," Solange said. "If DR did have money… DR made a lot of money, but he spent even more. Out of the two, I'd prefer that it was Lee who called me… I'd be sad that François had stooped so low."

"Sad but not surprised?"

Solange shook her head. "Nothing François does surprises me. He's desperate. He's terrified of Diane. If he did do something wrong and she finds out, she'll have his hide. Of course, the call might have come from Aymeric."

Ava pretended not to know the name. "Aymeric?"

"Aymeric Virgile… Marc Virgile's nephew. He's going to inherit the winery," Solange said with bitterness. "Aymeric knows nothing about wine. But he's a Virgile, and that's how the world works. In that respect, I understand Diane's anger. It wasn't fair that François got the winery. She's so much smarter than he is."

"Why would Aymeric want to scare you or be after DR's money?"

Solange shrugged. "I have no idea. I'm grasping at straws." She sipped her wine. "How is the book appraising going? Have you discovered any secret bank accounts?"

"Not yet," Ava replied, trying to appear light-hearted. "But there's always hope. Have you finished the inventory?"

"I'll finish today and then I'll drop off the keys at Garance's office. She's closing the shop. It's probably for the better." Solange poured them each more wine. "Thanks for listening. I probably sounded crazy. Now all we have to do is survive Marc's dinner. How hard can that be?"

Ava took a sip of wine. If things continued the way they were going, it might be very hard indeed.

CHAPTER 23

Reeling from what she had just learned, Ava kissed Solange on the cheeks as friends do and left the café. She walked down the rue des Abbesses toward the rue LePic, a long winding street that would bring her to the heights of Montmartre and the famous Place de Tertre. From there, she would go to DR's and see what she could find. But first, she needed to think.

Solange was upset. The phone call had shaken her. Ava knew that the caller wasn't mistaken. There was money, and it was missing. Anyone except Marc Virgile could have called Solange because Marc knew where the money was. Marc was the only one who could tell them why DR transferred all his money to a holding and had bought a parcel of land.

Halfway up the rue LePic, Ava slowed in front of one of the last wooden windmills in Montmartre. She took out her phone and snapped a photo. Van Gogh had made three paintings of the windmill in 1886. Back then, it had been surrounded by fields and hills rather than the white walled buildings that now lined the street.

As Ava snapped a second photo, there was movement behind her. She spun around. Someone dashed behind a delivery van. Ava bent over. A pair of men's feet was on the other side of the van.

Someone was following her.

Ava continued up the street as her heart beat faster and faster. No matter who it was, she was safe. There were loads of people out and about. All she had to do was scream. But first, she wanted to smoke the person out.

Strolling up to an art gallery, she pretended to study the painting in the window.

Instantly, François Croix dashed up to her and grabbed her arm. "We need to talk."

"Remove your hand, or I'll scream bloody murder," Ava said through clenched teeth.

As if burnt, François released her arm. "Sorry. I just wanted to get your attention."

"You succeeded. Why are you following me?"

François was astonished. "You saw me?"

Ava sighed. Lee was right. François was a bumbler. "A blind man would have seen you. What do you want?"

"Why were you having lunch with Solange?" François demanded, hands on his hips.

"Is that any of your business?"

"Yes… and no!" Nervous, François took out a vial of homeopathic pills and popped two in his mouth. "Ever since I got the email, I've been a nervous wreck. In fact, ever since DR died, I've been a nervous wreck."

"Tell me about it," Ava said and began walking toward the Place de Tertre.

"DR owed me money when he died."

"Why did he owe you money?"

"I sold him wine from my cellar. He promised to pay me a certain sum. He gave me half and told me I had to wait. I was furious and then he died." With a pained expression, François stared into Ava's eyes. "I need that money. If you help me find it, I'll give you 50%... No, 60%!"

Ava sighed. "If I could get my hands on DR's money, why would I give you part of it?"

François's shoulders slumped. "You wouldn't. I'm an idiot." He stood up straighter. "But you so seem like someone who would help a man who was at the end of his rope."

"Wrong," Ava said. "Did you ask Solange to help you?"

"I did. But she and I aren't on the best of terms."

"Why?"

"A gentlemen doesn't tell."

Ava shook her head. Not only was François a jerk, he was a chivalrous jerk. "Did you call her and threaten her?"

"Me? Did she say I did that?" François asked, raising his eyebrows in outrage.

Ava was mum.

"I did threaten her. But I didn't call her. I gave her the same deal I offered you."

"50%?" Ava asked. "What did she say?"

"She walked off without a word." François was upset. "I need the money. I don't know how to turn water into wine."

Ava was more and more puzzled.

Suddenly, François became angry. "There's only one way that this is going to end, but I don't know if I have the courage to do it!"

Alarmed, Ava reached out to him and touched his shoulder. "François, what do you mean!"

François pushed her hand away and stormed off down the street.

Watching him leave, Ava frowned. *Water into wine...* What in heaven's name did that mean?

CHAPTER 24

At DR's, Ava continued cataloguing the books. When she reached book two hundred and thirty, her phone rang. She looked at the number. It was Henri's.

"How was lunch?" Henri asked.

"Eventful. Someone threatened Solange over the phone yesterday evening. Give me the money, or you'll end up like DR…"

"What did she do?"

"That's why we had lunch. She thought it might be us."

"You and I?"

"I told her that was ridiculous. She admitted to a relationship with François. It was over a long time ago, but François won't accept that. He wants to get back with her. She also worries that tomorrow's dinner will end badly."

"I agree with her there."

"François followed me from the restaurant."

"Which means he followed Solange there."

"Something an obsessed ex would do. He was hopeless at trailing me. It was like he had a blinking red light over his head and a siren blaring."

"What did he want?"

"If I find the money, I should give it to him, and he'll give me 60%"

"Sounds like the deal of the century," Henri said with a chuckle.

"When I asked him about his relationship with Solange, he played the gentleman and refused to say anything. François did tell me that DR owed him money when he died and that he desperately needs it back.

"Maybe that's why he's worried about Diane. He's embezzled money."

"He also mumbled something about turning water into wine, an allusion that I don't get. When I refused his offer, he got angry and said there was only one way this was going to end but he didn't know if he had the courage to do it."

"Suicide?" Henri asked, alarmed.

"Suicide? François? That didn't even cross my mind. I see him murdering half of Montmartre before he'd touch a hair on his own head."

"Well, that's comforting," Henri joked. "I didn't learn anything we didn't know before. I'm having dinner with another friend this evening. Maybe I'll find out something then. Breakfast at Café Zola tomorrow. Text me if you find out anything in the meantime."

"Ditto." Ava hung up, perturbed. François was weak. Weak people do unpredictable things. She hoped he wouldn't do anything that would put his life, or someone else's life, in jeopardy."

Ava worked another five hours. She deserved a gold medal for all the books she had gone through. Unfortunately, none of them held any clues. Ava put the books back on the shelves and got ready to leave. Like the day before, she did a walk around the apartment to see if there was anything she had missed.

She made her way through the living room, opening drawers and closing them. She picked up cushions and shook them. She did the same thing in the alcove. Striding into the kitchen, she opened drawers and cabinets and searched the refrigerator.

And then she saw it.

It was something she should have noticed the first time. Well, she did notice it the first time, but she hadn't understand its significance.

Why would DR who didn't cook have a large coffee table cookbook in his kitchen?

Ava picked the heavy cookbook up and opened it. Handwritten papers were inside it. Ava took one and read it As she did, her hand began to shake. She grabbed another paper. Like the first one, mathematical computations were written on it along with letters. 1/8 LL1. 1/3 BS 3… They were the same numbers she had seen on each shelf under the rows of bottles at the French Corkscrew.

Barely able to breathe, Ava removed all the papers and stuffed them in her handbag. When her phone rang, she answered immediately. "Henri?"

Instead of Henri's voice, a deep male voice spoke. The voice sounded panicked "Where are you? We have to see each other."

It took her a second to recognize Aymeric's voice. "Aymeric, what's wrong? I'm at DR's."

"I'm not sure what's wrong. Meet me at the bottom of the funicular. I have to go."

Ava stuck her phone in her handbag and began to run.

CHAPTER 25

Aymeric was pacing nervously back and forth on the edge of the crowd near the flower kiosk. The moment Ava stepped out of the funicular car, he dashed toward her. He was in a panic, sweating and unable to get his words out. "I didn't know who to call. I thought of you."

Ava was astonished by his state. "What is it?"

He caught his breath and began to speak. "Solange… I followed her today. I saw you having lunch.

"What else did you see?" Ava asked, frowning. There certainly was a parade of people following other people today. Who else had seen her lunching with Solange?

"After Solange left the café, I followed her back to the shop. I hung around down the street. She hasn't seen me in a long time. Since I used to have a beard, I felt safe hanging around nearby. Then François dropped in."

"What time was this?" Ava asked, trying to draw up a timeline of events.

"About an hour after you left the restaurant."

Ava's mind raced. So immediately after François wondered if he'd have the courage to do something, he went to see Solange.

"When they walked outside, they were arguing. I was worried they'd see me and moved down the street," Aymeric said. "A few minutes later, François stormed off. He was furious."

"Where did he go?" Ava asked, sure that this was important.

Aymeric shrugged. "I don't know. There's only one of me. I decided to keep following Solange. Forty minutes later, she made a call on her cell phone and then went to François's building."

Ava was surprised. "How do you know his address?"

"I knew he had an apartment in Paris. I looked up his address on the web."

"Was François there?"

"Again, I don't know. I was outside. Solange didn't stay long… ten minutes at the most. But then the most astounding thing happened…" Aymeric stopped to catch his breath. "Guess who she went to see?"

"I'm not good at guessing games. Just tell me," Ava replied, annoyed at Aymeric's disjointed storytelling ability.

"Roger," Aymeric announced with a dramatic wave of his hand.

"Roger Allard?!" Ava said, flabbergasted.

"The very same. They met in a café. He kissed her on the lips before putting his arm around her. Then he took her hand in his..."

Ava couldn't believe what she was hearing. "What else?"

"I couldn't get too close, Roger knows me. They spoke for over a half hour. Solange was weeping. Every now and then Roger ran his hand through her hair. He took her chin in his hand and tried to kiss her. She pushed him away. Roger looked worried. Solange was angry. When Solange left, I followed her back to her apartment on the rue des Abbesses. I waited an hour. When she didn't come out, I called you."

Ava felt feverish. The new information was so startling, she didn't know what it meant.

Aymeric shook his head. "Something is happening. Something major. I don't know what that is... It's like time is speeding up. Something is going to happen before my uncle's dinner."

"Why did you call me?"

"I didn't know who else to call. I thought you and Henri could help me. But I only had your phone number. You are detectives, aren't you?"

Ava frowned. "Where did you learn that?"

"From George.. My uncle's driver. My uncle tells George everything. George would never breathe a word of this. But when my uncle was pushed into traffic, George began to worry. I had breakfast with him this morning and he told me about you and Henri. I also managed to get the keys to the

French Corkscrew," Aymeric said, holding up a set of keys.

"You have the keys to the shop?"

Aymeric took a key ring out of his pocket and held it up. "I do!"

Ava beamed. "Aymeric, I could kiss you."

Aymeric shook his head. "I'd prefer that we solved the case first."

"I was speaking metaphorically," Ava said with a shake of her head.

The sun was setting, and the bottom of the butte was cast in shadows. After waiting until the street was empty, Aymeric and Ava hurried to the shop. Aymeric unlocked the door and they slipped inside. Aymeric locked the door behind them.

The tall trees across the road meant that the shop was dark. As Ava went around pulling the shades down making the shop even darker, Aymeric turned on the lights and walked around.

"So this is the infamous French Corkscrew." He strode over to the shelves and picked up bottles at random and read the labels. "I'm disappointed. Where are the fabulous wines DR was known for?"

Her heart beating, Ava walked up to the shelf and looked at the numbers that were taped in front of each row of wines: LL1… BB3… LL2…

Ava opened her bag and took out one of the papers from the cookbook. She strode to the other shelves and eyed the numbers written there.

Seeing the paper in her hand, Aymeric frowned. "What's that?"

"A paper I found at DR's…"

Aymeric took it from her and knitted his eyebrows together as he read it. "DK7 = (22 ml, LL1)+ (4ml, RS3)+50ml, TI6) It reads. like a recipe."

"It's how DR turned water into wine."

Hearing a noise, Aymeric spun around. It was a scooter backfiring in the street. He handed the paper back to her and glanced around the shop. "We have to hurry. Solange might come back. I want to check out the cellar." He moved to the cellar door and opened it. He turned on the light and started down the steps.

Remembering that Solange had warned that the door locks when shut, Ava went to the hook next to the door. The key wasn't there. Ava propped the door open with a case of wine and went down the steps slowly. When she reached the bottom, Aymeric was walking around the perimeter of the cellar inspecting the walls.

"We're down really deep. We must be next to the quarries." Aymeric frowned, puzzled. "Where's the wine?"

"There isn't any…. Except for a few bottles in the corner," Ava said as she pointed at a few unlabeled bottles on a wooden table near the crates of notebooks.

Aymeric sighed. "I'm disappointed. I'd secretly hoped that DR had a fabulous wine collection stashed away here."

Ava moved to the three crates in the corner and looked in the first one. It was filled with school notebooks and pencils.

"This reminds me of my school days," Aymeric said as he joined her.

"Help me move this. I want to see the crate underneath."

Ava lifted one side of the crate while Aymeric lifted the other. They placed it on the floor. The second crate was filled with empty wine bottles.

"Look at the bottom of the bottles. They're really old. They don't make bottles like this any more," Aymeric said pointing at the base of the dark green bottles.

Lost in thought, Ava raised her eyebrows. "Doesn't it strike you as strange that DR has old empty bottles in his cellar?"

Aymeric shook his head. "No stranger than having old school notebooks."

"I want to see the crate on the bottom," Ava said.

Together, they lifted the crate with the bottles up and slid it onto the floor. The third crate was filled with old paper. Aymeric stuck his hand into the jumble of paper and pulled a few pieces out. They were all blank except for one that had a wine label printed on it: Domaine de Kirjac 2000. The name of the winery was crooked and the ink was smudged.

"Domaine de Kirjac 2000. I was right," Aymeric whispered, stunned. Realizing the significance of his words, he went white and murmured, "My uncle was involved... What am I going to do?"

Before Ava could respond, there was a loud banging noise at the top of the steps. In a flash, Ava sprinted toward them. She dashed up them just in time to hear a key turn in the lock. Ava banged on the door. "Let us out! Let us out!

The cellar lights went out. Ava hit the switch next to her. Nothing happened. "Someone's turned off the lights."

Using the flashlight on his phone to guide him, Aymeric joined her. He pushed on the door. He kicked it. "This is solid wood. We won't be able to break it down." He looked at his phone. "I don't have a network."

Ava checked her phone. "I don't have one either. What are we going to do?"

Aymeric began to hammer on the door and shout. Ava walked back down to the cellar. Someone had locked them in. No one would find them because no one knew they were there and Garance was shutting the shop.

Covered in sweat, Aymeric came down the steps. "It's no use. No one can hear us. We need to wait until tomorrow until there are people in the streets." Using his flashlight to light the way, he walked to the table in the corner and picked up a bottle of wine. Using a corkscrew on his keychain, he opened it.

"Are you always so prepared?" Ava asked as she sat

down on the crate with the notebooks.

"When you work in wine, you have a corkscrew with you all the time."

"Did you tell your uncle's driver that you were coming her?"

"No. I swiped the keys when he wasn't looking. Someone will find us sooner or later."

Ava sighed. "It's the later that worries me. Turn off your flashlight. We need to save our batteries."

Aymeric turned his flashlight off. They were plunged into darkness. It took a few minutes for Ava's eyes to adjust.

"When you don't show up tomorrow, people will come looking for you," Aymeric said. He reached out, took the bottle of wine, wiped the top of the bottle with his shirt and sipped it. "This is a Domaine de Kirjac 2000. The real stuff… How did DR get his hands on it?"

Water into wine, Ava thought.

Unable to sleep, Ava shivered from the dampness. As her shoulder was numb, she shifted her position against the wall. Aymeric was seated on a crate next to her. He was asleep. Ava closed her eyes and attempted to stop her mind from racing. This would be a wonderful story to tell if they got out alive…

The lights were blinding. Dazed, Ava opened her eyes. Hearing the sound of footsteps on the stairs, Aymeric jumped to his feet and grabbed a bottle of wine, ready to defend himself. When Henri and Marc Virgile reached the cellar, Aymeric lowered the bottle.

"What took you so long?" Aymeric asked his uncle.

Marc eyed his nephew and sighed. "A thank you for coming out in the middle of the night would be welcome."

Ava stood up and smiled gratefully. "Thank you. I was worried no one would find us. What time is it?"

"3 am," Marc replied as he looked around the cellar.

"How did you find us?" Ava asked Henri.

"Nate was worried when you didn't call him. He called me and mentioned that you intended to break into the shop. I called Marc who had a set of keys, and here we are."

Tears welled up in Ava's eyes. She was lucky to have Nate and Henri in her life.

Marc eyed the label on the table next to the wine. He didn't say anything. "There's something you should know. François tried to kill himself. He took pills. Luckily, he was running a bath, and it flooded the neighbor's apartment. Otherwise, they wouldn't have found him in time."

Ava frowned. *Why run a bath if you were planning to kill yourself?* "Will he make it?"

"Probably not," Henri replied. "It's no one's fault, Ava."

"What are we going to do now?" Aymeric asked as he eyed the bottle of wine in his hand. The remark was aimed at his uncle and encompassed more than just François's attempted suicide.

"Go home and get some sleep," Marc said. "Tomorrow is the tasting."

"You're not going to go through with it?" Aymeric asked his uncle, in disbelief.

"I owe it to DR…" Marc replied.

Ava sat in the back of Marc's car with Henri and Aymeric, while Marc rode in the front next to his driver. As Aymeric's hotel was in Montmartre, he was the first person dropped off.

Ava eyed Henri. She had a million questions for him but couldn't ask them in front of the others.

When the car neared Ava's apartment, Marc turned to Henri and Ava. "With everything that's happened, I've decided to shake things up a bit."

Henri stared at Marc. "Is that wise?"

Marc raised his eyebrows. "Wise? No. Necessary? Yes. I'll be holding the sale tomorrow at noon."

"At your friend's mansion?" Henri asked.

Marc shook his head. "At the French Corkscrew."

Silent, Henri nodded.

When the car pulled up in front of Ava's, she kissed Henri on the cheek and slipped him one of the pieces of paper she had found in the cookbook. "I want to thank both of you for saving me. Freezing to death in a wine cellar is not the best way to die. "At least, you had good wine to drink," Marc said with a look that spoke for itself. "It's not often that you can find a Domaine de Kirjac 2000."

EPILOGUE

The French Corkscrew was bathed in light. The sun was streaming through the windows when Ava entered the shop. Marc Virgile walked up to her and greeted her. "You're the first one. That must be your English punctuality."

Ava was disappointed that Henri wasn't there. She had tried to call him when she got home last night, but he hadn't answered his phone. She had called him the first thing this morning and he had texted her back that he would see her at the shop.

"How is François?"

"It doesn't look good," Marc said. "Would you like a coffee?"

Ava nodded and followed him to the back of the shop where he made them both a coffee using DR's espresso machine.

As she walked past the shelves, she froze. The papers

that had been under the bottles last night had been removed. All that was left was rows of wine. Ava turned to him. "You've tidied up the shop."

"I took care of loose ends," Marc said as he handed her a coffee. "I had breakfast with my nephew this morning. He understands things better now."

Before Ava could ask him what those things were, the door opened, and Lee Baresi strode toward them.

"How is François?" Lee asked in a low pained voice.

"How did you learn about it?" Ava asked, puzzled.

"It was in Marc's text telling us to meet here at noon," Lee replied.

With a sad sigh, Marc shook his head. "He probably won't make it."

Lee clenched his jaw.

Solange entered the shop. She was visibly distraught, and her eyes were red. Clearly, she had been weeping. Holding back a sob, she spoke, "I can't believe François would do something so..." She paused as she looked for the right word. "Stupid."

Diane de la Floch walked toward them accompanied by Roger Allard. Diane was dressed all in black. She was totally chic, as usual. She also had red eyes.

Roger spoke directly to Marc. "The prognosis?"

Marc shook his head.

"François didn't try and kill himself. I can't believe it," Diane said.

"It's my fault. We had a fling when I was writing my book. He came by the shop yesterday and begged me to take him back. I refused. He said I'd regret it…" Solange said as she burst into tears. Her whole body began to shake.

Ava eyed Roger. He was ill-at-ease, while Solange didn't even glance at him. *Was Aymeric wrong? Had he misread the situation?*

"Solange, if François did try and commit suicide, it's not because of you. He could never love anyone more than himself," Diane said in a poor attempt at comforting the woman.

Solange sniffled. "You're wrong. He adored me. I pushed him to it."

"Maybe it's about the money…" Lee said.

Diane froze and raised her eyebrows. "Pray tell…"

Marc sighed. "François had been selling bottles from your winery's cellar and his wife's cellar to DR for a while. When he learned the prices the wine had been sold for, he wanted a bigger cut. He threatened DR."

"And then DR fell down the stairs," Diane said.

Lee nodded. "And then DR fell down the stairs."

"François and DR had it out the night of DR's death. But François would never have hurt DR. François is not that type of man," Solange said.

"If you'd broken up, how did you know that?" Diane asked.

"Because we spent the night together afterward," Solange said.

"What time was that?" Lee asked.

"Around 2 am. We'd had dinner in Pigalle. It was raining. We ran into DR in the street, and they started arguing," Solange said.

"What did you do?" Lee asked.

"I went back to my apartment and waited," Solange said.

"What time did François get there?" Henri asked as he walked across the shop.

Ava looked up at him. She wondered why he had gotten to the shop late. Henri was never late unless there was a good reason for it."

"An hour later…" Solange said as her shoulders slumped. She began to weep again.

Marc looked from one to the other. "I know the timing is off but we're here to talk about my wine."

Solange became hysterical. "François is going to die, and all you care about is wine… You're like DR. You're cold and inhuman."

Henri stepped forward. "I've just come from the hospital. There's been a change in François's condition." He dialed a number on his cell phone and put it on speaker phone. The number rang.

Everyone stared at the phone.

"I have good news for you. I'm going to be fine," François said.

Diane went pale. Roger looked at Solange with sadness. Lee and Ava were flabbergasted. Only Marc and Henri weren't surprised.

"Someone put sleeping pills in my whiskey… If Roger hadn't come by, I would have died."

Furious, Solange wheeled around and shoved Roger with all her force. "Traitor! You said you loved me." Pushing everyone aside, she ran to the door and left.

"Stop her!" Ava shouted as she bounded after Solange.

Roger grabbed Ava's arm and shook his head. "She won't get far. She's no longer a danger to anyone."

Outraged, Ava eyed Henri. "Aren't you going to call the police?"

Henri shook his head. "François doesn't want to."

"Because he killed DR?" Ava asked.

"Because it was Solange who ran after DR that night. She argued with him on the steps. He fell and hit his head," Henri said.

"I don't believe that," Ava said.

"We don't have any proof that Solange killed DR," Roger

said.

"She tried to kill François," Ava insisted.

"She was angry that I wouldn't get back with her," François responded.

Ava stared at the phone. "She left you!"

"I left her. She wouldn't accept it," François said.

Roger nodded. "She was obsessed with François. Solange and I had a brief relationship. I fell in love with her. But once she met François, I didn't exist. I waited. I was patient. When I saw her yesterday she talked about making François pay for what he did. Later, I was worried and went to his apartment. I saw him lying on the floor of his apartment from the window in the hallway. The concierge opened the door and we called an ambulance."

"Then there was no overflowing bathtub?" Ava asked.

Roger shook his head no.

Ava looked at the phone again. "François, why did you go see Solange yesterday after you spoke to me?"

François responded, "To blackmail her into finding me DR's money. I needed it…"

Diane stood up straight. "When you're out of the hospital we need to talk. I'll give you the money to pay back your ex-wife and the winery. You, of course, will leave the winery. In exchange, I'll help you find a position for you far from France and me."

François was silent.

"Then we agree?" Diane asked.

"Yes, I agree," François said defeated.

Diane smiled.

"Someone locked Aymeric and I in the cellar yesterday. Who did it?" Ava asked.

"Solange probably," Lee said quickly.

Ava stared at Lee, suspicious. If it had been him, then he had time to see the numbers under the wine and what each wine was. But did he have the "recipes?

"And the person who scared me at DR's the other day?" Ava asked.

Silence.

François spoke. "It was me. I knocked on the door. No one answered so I used a key I had to get in. I startled you and you fell."

Ava was outraged. "Why didn't you help me."

"I was scared. I checked your pulse. It was OK. I left. Then I worried that you were hurt. I went back and was starting up the stairs when I heard you and Aymeric talking. I had to run out of the building and hide," François explained. "I'm sorry. I have to go as the nurse is here." He hung up.

Marc turned to Roger. "What are you going to do with Solange?"

Roger smiled sadly. "Find her. Get her help. I love her, but it's too late for that. There's no fool like an old fool."

"And the sale?" Lee asked, all business.

Diane shook her head. "I'll be taking over the winery. I withdraw as a potential buyer as does François."

"I'm out. I have something more important things to take care of," Roger said.

Marc looked at Lee.

Lee smiled. "Name your price!"

"Then that's settled," Marc said.

"What about the money DR sent to you? Where is it?" Ava asked staring at Marc.

Henri spoke. "DR wanted to open his foundation. Marc learned about a parcel of land that was for sale. The owner wanted to sell quickly and quietly for cash."

Marc nodded. "We bought it. DR was sure he could make a large profit reselling it. He was right. I sent the money back to Singapore yesterday. It's a tragedy about Solange. DR left instructions that she was to run the foundation,"

"What will happen to it now?" Diane asked.

"As I'm handing over the reins to Aymeric, I'll have time to set it up as DR had planned," Marc said. "There's nothing like a new venture to keep you young."

"Who sent the invitation to the tasting?" Ava asked.

Marc raised his hand. "DR and I had planned the tasting together. When he died, I decided to continue on."

"And the email address?" Diane asked.

"I created it… It's not his usual email address," Marc said.

"Did he really say that he suspected that one of us was trying to kill him?" Lee asked.

"No. I made that up… Maybe in the back of my mind, I suspected one of you as you were all here at the time he died."

"I'm going to be leaving you," Diane said. "I have a lot to do."

Roger also turned to leave. "I need to find Solange."

Both left.

Lee shifted from foot to foot. "I'm off. He eyed the shelves. Too bad that some things had to end."

Marc was silent.

Ava, Henri and Marc were the last ones in the shop.

Marc sank onto a stool and remained silent as he looked around the shop.

"Can you tell us what happened?" Henri asked.

Marc nodded. "Between us?"

"Between us," Henri replied.

"I met DR years ago. He came to ask me to sell him some older vintages of Domaine de Kirjac. Unfortunately, my father has sold most of them off and there weren't many bottles left, although few people knew that. DR had promised a case of 1977 wine to a client. When I told him there was almost none left, he had an idea…"

"Water into wine?" Ava asked.

"Ordinary wine into Domaine de Kirjac," Marc responded. "I accepted. He tasted a bottle of 1977 and then recreated it. No. I should say he created it. I couldn't taste the difference. I helped him with the labels. And then the winery had a year that we lost almost all the wine…"

Henri raised his eyebrows. "And he helped you again?"

"Yes," Marc said. "But then, I decided not to tempt fate. I stopped."

"Did DR create other wines?" Ava asked.

"Yes. But he also had decided to stop. When François discovered that some of the wines he had sold to DR had been auctioned off in higher quantities, François threatened him. DR took that as a sign."

Ava frowned. "Was Solange involved?"

Marc shook his head. "No. She knew nothing about it. She was angry with DR because she thought he had lied to her about the foundation. He hadn't, of course. He was just trying to put as much money as possible aside."

"Why did she argue with him the night he died?" Henri asked.

"DR is the only one who can answer that. I miss him," Marc said with a tear in his eye.

Ava took the recipes out of her handbag. "What about these?"

Marc took a piece of paper and looked at it. "I looked for them everywhere. Where were they?"

"In a cookbook in the kitchen," Ava said.

Marc waved his hands at the shelves. "Wine creation is over. I removed the papers and shuffled them."

Henri looked puzzled. "Why?"

"So I wouldn't be tempted…" Marc answered. "All things have an end." He walked to a shelf and brought over a decanter of wine and an empty bottle of Domaine de Kirjac 1997. "I opened it earlier." Marc poured the wine into three glasses as Henri examined the empty bottle.

"Is this the real thing?" Ava asked.

"We'll never know," Marc replied. He raised his glass in the air. "To DR!"

"To DR!" Henri and Ava said.

As Ava sipped the wine, a smile spread across her face. She wondered what Proust would have said about the wine. For Ava, it was great. Absolutely great.

PREVIEW OF *DEATH ON THE QUAI*

It was the best of times, it was the worst of times, and it was only Thursday…

Curled up in bed, Ava Sext watched the rain bounce off her apartment's glass roof. The raindrops fell in a repetitive manner and made a hypnotic pinging sound as they hit the glass. It was a summer rain -- a rain that was welcome after the long string of stiflingly hot days that Paris had been experiencing.

The weather report had predicted rain only for late this afternoon. But what did the weather report know? It had started raining in the middle of the night and hadn't stopped since.

It didn't matter when the rain had started. The downpour meant that Ava, who sold used books from an outdoor stand overlooking the Seine, had a reason to stay home and do nothing until it stopped.

Listening to the sound of the raindrops cheered her. By the time she got to her stand, the air would be crisp and clean. The leaves on the trees on the quay below would appear greener. The cobblestones along the river would glisten in the sunlight. The Seine would flow by, revitalized by this manna from heaven.

Summer rain was a gift. It was not something to complain about.

Not wanting to waste an instant, Ava pulled her long frame out of bed and stretched her arms high in the air as she slipped her feet into her bluebird blue Moroccan slippers.

Striding across the loft apartment that had once been a series of maids' rooms, she slowed in front of the record player to choose an album from her late uncle's collection of 60's and 70's rock. After hesitating between Judy Collins and Steppenwolf, she chose the latter. What she needed was music to jog her awake.

She carefully placed the needle on her favorite song. As the first notes of "Born to be Wild" rang through the apartment, she headed to the kitchen with new spring in her step.

Almost dancing, she took a package of special ground Italian coffee off a shelf and measured it out. She put it in an espresso maker, added water and turned on the gas burner.

Looking down, she noticed that Mercury's bowl was still full. He had decided to skip breakfast. Ava didn't know what the cat's name really was. She called him Mercury because, like the planet, he appeared most mornings. He'd slip into the apartment through an open window and head straight to the kitchen. Mercury was black with slanted green eyes. He was well fed and well groomed. For some reason, he had decided that it was her job to give him breakfast. For all she knew, her place just might be one stop on his breakfast tour of the neighborhood.

Ava had learned one thing from their brief relationship -- Mercury was a fair weather cat. He didn't appear on rainy days, snowy days (not that there were many of them in Paris) or on windy days.

As the strong aroma of brewing coffee filled the kitchen, Ava inhaled deeply. She poured some coffee into her favorite mug: the one with the Union Jack Flag on it. For the briefest of moments, a ripple of homesickness ran through her.

Ava was a transplanted Londoner who had lived in Paris less than a year.

She owed her presence in the city to her late Uncle Charles. After receiving a large inheritance, Charles Sext, a New Scotland Yard detective, had quit the force and moved to France to run an outdoor book stand in Paris, having decided to enjoy life far from crime and criminals with a glass of good Bordeaux and as many books as he could read.

When Charles died, he left Ava his apartment in Paris and a monthly stipend on the condition that she lived there for a year.

More than money, her uncle had left her a philosophy: *Take time to live life.*

For Ava, good coffee was an important part of living life. It was also the first step to a perfect day.

Sitting at the large wooden table that separated the kitchen from the rest of the apartment, she sipped her coffee slowly, savoring its earthy flavor.

Reflecting on her time in Paris, she liked to think that she had become a little bit Parisian. For one thing, she complained about the weather. London's weather was far worse than Paris's weather, but Londoners didn't complain about it. They took it in stride. If a tornado swept through Trafalgar Square, Ava was sure that many London residents would ignore it and go about their day.

In Paris, complaining about the weather was standard conversational fare. Rain or shine, it was the one subject that Parisians always circled back to. Ava suspected that it had very little to do with the weather and a lot to do with the complainer's outlook on life.

Just yesterday, Ava had bought a crispy *baguette* for dinner at her local *boulangerie*. When she had commented on the beautiful weather, the woman selling bread had frowned and had shaken her head ominously.

"It's nice today, but tomorrow who knows?" the woman said, arching her eyebrows as if a tsunami was about to hit Paris.

For some inexplicable reason, Ava had an urge to complain about today's rain. It was like an itch she couldn't scratch. She wondered what it meant.

Checking the time, she saw that it was too late to call Benji in New York. Benji was a doctoral student in medieval manuscripts. They had had a brief whirlwind romance. It wasn't a romance that made fireworks go off. It was what the French call "*une amitié amoureuse*", a romantic friendship.

Whatever you called it, Benji had done wonders for her morale. But he was in New York, she was in Paris, and neither of them had any desire to change that.

Last week, when Benji had suggested that it was time to move on, Ava hadn't disagreed with him. As long as she could keep the friendship part of their romantic friendship, she was fine.

Restless, she stood up and poured herself more coffee, taking care to leave some for later.

Sipping it, she frowned. It wasn't the rain or the end of her relationship with Benji that was bothering her. It was something more deep-seated.

She paced over to the record player, picked the needle up and put it back on the track "Born to be Wild". Listening to the lyrics, a feverish agitation bubbled up inside her.

What she needed was excitement.

She needed something *inattendu* to happen... something totally unexpected.

In London, she would have said she was bored. But this was Paris, home of Sartre and Simone de Beauvoir, philosophers who had sipped cocktails at *Les Deux Magots* café while chain smoking and speaking about existentialism: the confusion of the individual when faced with the meaninglessness of the modern world.

What Ava was experiencing was an existential crisis.

Why was she alive?

What was she going to do with her life?

Did life even have meaning?

Ava needed the heavens to open and shoot lightning bolts from the sky to shake her from this crisis of nothingness that she had fallen into.

What she needed for lack of a better term was a "somethingness".

When she had accepted the conditions in her late uncle's will, what had tipped the balance was having time to figure out what she wanted to do with her life.

Ava didn't regret for an instant leaving her London job in a boutique PR firm where her days and nights had been devoted to posting social media posts for celebrity clients.

She loved selling books. She loved Paris. But most of all, she loved sleuthing -- a talent she shared with her late uncle.

Ava had only worked on a few cases, but she had quickly discovered that sleuthing was exciting, intellectually stimulating and adrenaline-packed.

It was also highly addictive.

Perhaps, what lay at the heart of her existential crisis was that she was a crime-junkie waiting for a crime to happen.

It didn't have to be murder.

It could be fraud, blackmail or even petty theft.

Instead, it was raining.

If someone asked her about the rain in her present state of mind, she would tell them that after the rain came the sun.

And that was what she needed… a sunny adventure to light up her life.

Looking up, Ava saw that the rain had stopped.

It was time to get dressed.

She finished her coffee and put the cup in the sink. Then, she walked to the record player and moved the needle back to listen to "Born to be Wild" one last time for inspiration.

Suddenly, a ray of dazzling sunshine burst through the glass roof and lit up the apartment. If this were a film instead of a book, Ava would have heard the earth shake and the heavens roar. She might even have heard the trumpeting of angels' horns.

Instead, she heard her doorbell ring.

Or didn't.

As she crossed the apartment, she heard a strange knocking sound. Turning, she eyed the pipes in the kitchen. They had a habit of knocking when the next-door neighbor ran his washing machine.

It took her a few seconds to realize that the knocking wasn't coming from the pipes. It was coming from her front door.

"I'm on my way," Ava shouted as she turned the music off. The sound of knocking and the tinny ringing sound of her doorbell now echoed through the apartment. After a quick inspection of what she was wearing -- flowered pajama bottoms and a rock concert T-shirt -- she headed to the door.

Turning the key twice in the lock, she unlocked the door and swung it open.

A tiny woman, soaked from head to foot, was standing on Ava's doormat. The woman had a pen in one hand and a business card in the other. Two cameras were slung across her chest.

Seeing Ava, the woman pushed her curly damp hair behind her ear, smiled and waved the business card in the air. "I was just writing you a note. I'm so lucky that you answered the door!"

Lucky!

A shiver of anticipation ran through Ava.

This was a sign.

Hearing a loud meowing behind her, Ava turned.

Mercury was standing there staring at the woman with suspicion.

When it rains, it pours…

SERIES INFORMATION

The Paris Booksellers Mysteries are light-hearted cozy mysteries that plunge you into the joys and tribulations of living in Paris, where food, wine and crime make life worth living… along with a book or two.

Books in the series are stand-alones and can be read in any order.

Death on the Seine Book 1
Death in the Louvre Book 2
Death on the Quai Book 3
Death in Montmartre Book 4

A Little Paris Christmas Murder is a 90 minute holiday short read in the series.

Evan Hirst also writes the *Isa Floris* thrillers that blend together far-flung locations, ancient secrets and fast-paced action in an intriguing mix of fact and fiction aimed at keeping you on the edge of your seat.

The Aquarius Prophecy
The Paradise Betrayal

Find out more about Evan Hirst's books at

www.evanhirst.com

Made in the USA
Middletown, DE
23 April 2019